grow & glow

The Fizz Sisters' guide to being happy, healthy, and glowing from the inside out while growing up

Mia Fizz & Sienna Fizz

xoxo

Copyright © 2024 by Mia Fizz & Sienna Fizz

All rights reserved. This book or any portion thereof may not be reproduced or used in any manner whatsoever without the express written permission of the publisher except for the use of brief quotations in a book review.

© Text by
Mia Fizz & Sienna Fizz, 2024

© Photographs by
Mia Fizz, Lauren Marsh, 2024

Edited by Stacy K

Designed by
Anna Perotti | bythebookdesign.com

First Printing, 2024

ISBN 978-1-9163004-3-9

Contents

8 **Introduction**

20 **Chapter One:** glowing up

44 **Chapter Two:** thoughts become things

58 **Chapter Three:** becoming a young adult

66 **Chapter Four:** the puberty chapter

80 **Chapter Five:** friendship & crushes

92 **Chapter Six:** eat to glow

108 **Chapter Seven:** all about family

120 **Chapter Eight:** finding your passion

130 **Chapter Nine:** in your sporty era

144 **Chapter Ten:** learning and growing

156 **Chapter Eleven:** travel to grow

175 the end

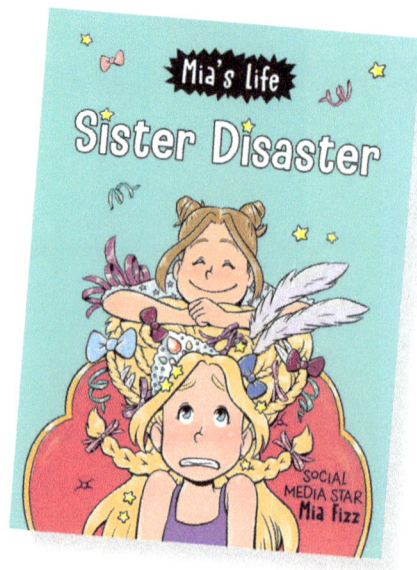

PREVIOUSLY BY MIA FIZZ

Awkward to Awesome

All Things Mia Fizz Coloring Book

Mia's Life: Fan Takeover!

Mia's Life: Best Friends for Never

Mia's Life: Sister Disaster!

Introduction

Mia **Hey, I'm Mia.** You may recognise me from my family's social media accounts (We're almost at ten million followers between us across the social medias now!), or from my previous book, *Awkward to Awesome,* which I self-published at fourteen and quickly became an Amazon best-seller. I'm nineteen years old, the oldest of four, and I love writing and making videos in the hope that it can help at least one person make their life a little better. I wrote my previous book with that same intention, and all the reviews and feedback meant so much to me, because you told me that I had actually helped! I've learnt so much more in the time since then, so I realised that I really wanted to make a standalone Part 2. But I knew that I needed something extra special for this book, when it hit me. Watching my little sister grow up has been one of the best experiences in my life, and it's crazy to me that the girl I remember as a toddler is now a thirteen-year-old! She's so thoughtful, kind, and dedicated, and one of my biggest inspirations. I know the world has so much to learn from her, so it was obvious what we had to do: write this book together! It has been such a bonding experience for us, and I'm so proud of Sienna for all the work she put into this, I have to say this is the best book *ever.*

Sienna **Hey! I'm Sienna.** I've always wanted to find the perfect book for tweens and teens, so it is a dream come true that now that I'm actually a teen myself, I've written one! But of course, I couldn't have done it by myself, so my big sister, Mia, is the perfect partner. I've always looked up to Mia because she's always been the cool, fun big sis I wanted, and we have so many nice memories together. To get to know me a bit, here are some fun facts about me:

- I'm a level 5 gymnast, and I absolutely LOVE gymnastics (as you will probably notice while reading this book).

- My fave food is Tex-Mex (a full feast with a burrito, tacos, and lots of salsa!)

- My fave colours are pink and blue because I really can't decide between the two.

- I love sunbathing at the beach and swimming in the sea.

- My fave aesthetics are coquette and coconut girl.

- My fave subject is English (not including PE and art).

Mia   Me and Sienna have so many good memories together, but here are some of my faves:

When Sienna was a newborn.

We're both so little, he-he.

11

This is when we went to the famous Santa Monica beach in Los Angeles, California.

12

Filming one of our first ever Fizz Sisters YouTube videos!

At the beach in Bali, Indonesia.

*We were in a
magazine together.
Can you see us on
the cover?*

We did a Family Fizz show!

15

We went to this super-cute clothing brand event in London.

And this is us writing this very book!

Anyways, enough about us.

Welcome to *Grow and Glow*. We came up with this book name because of the viral trend on social media of "glow ups". Usually for this trend people focus on "glowing up" superficially, like getting a spray tan or a new haircut, and while this is fun, and we have included some of our fave fashion and beauty tips, that's not really what this book is about. This book is about glowing from the inside out. Discovering what gets you feeling motivated. Becoming the healthiest, happiest, and most radiating version of yourself. Becoming a better friend, daughter, or sibling. But most of all, becoming your best self while growing up.

To make sure you know who's talking in each section, we've added an *S* for Sienna and an *M* for Mia next to each paragraph. Also, throughout the book, we've included our answers to some of the actual questions our followers asked us on our social medias.

We hope you enjoy reading this book as much as we enjoyed writing it! xoxo

glowing up

xoxo

1

> *How do you gain confidence to stop wearing makeup every day?* **BY SOPHIE**

I used to wear makeup pretty much every day, and I loved it. Putting my makeup on was often my favourite part of my morning routine. I love how you get the power to decide what style you're going to do every day, and how it can complete an outfit. On the flip side, I think it's really important to be aware of what you're putting onto your skin. After seeing some people speak out about it online, I paused and decided to actually check out the back of those bottles for myself. It was quite scary to see what was really in them! Thankfully, more and more people are becoming aware and there's been a lot of exposure on brands which have been putting toxic chemicals which are *proven* to be harmful into "beauty" products for years. As a result, there are more and more brands popping up every day with clean, safe-to-use, natural products. I'd strongly recommend having a sort through your products and try to use only truly natural ones. It's taken me a few years to finally get the point where I can say I'm pretty much chemical-free, so don't worry if you can't make an immediate change, but every little thing you swap, the better. However, the main reason I wanted to quit makeup is because while it's super fun to play with, it is also so easy to get trapped in a cycle of always wearing it and forgetting about your natural beauty. I knew I needed to do something about it when I realised how insecure I felt whenever I didn't wear mascara (which was very *very* rarely). I have really light blonde lashes, and I've always been aware of that and didn't like how they looked naturally. The more I thought about it, the more I realised that the only reason I felt that way is that the current beauty standard is to have long, dark lashes. There is absolutely nothing wrong with having blonde lashes, and you can look beautiful with them. In fact, I realised that light lashes suit me way more since they are meant to go with the rest of my features. I had gotten so caught up in trying to look like everybody else that I forgot to look like me. I decided that the only way to change the fact that I didn't like how I looked without mascara was to go cold turkey and completely quit. Don't get me wrong, it was hard at first. Every photo I took of myself I disliked, and I felt as if I was half-dressed every day. But I kid you not, after about two weeks maximum, I was completely used to and appreciated how I look naturally. Now I feel more confident than ever in the skin I was born with, and even if I do decide to start wearing makeup again, I'll truly know and believe that I am just as beautiful without it.

M Here are some of my favourite natural glow-up tips that make me feel more confident and glowing every day:

- *Healthy hair and lashes* I like to use organic castor oil on my eyelashes and eye area every night. It's super moisturising and helps your lashes grow super long. I also use it as a hair mask with rosemary sometimes, as they both stimulate hair growth.

- *Considering my skin's good bacteria* If you use harsh products on the skin, you're actually disrupting the natural balance of your microbiome (the good bacteria that lives on and in your body), which can cause serious problems in the long term. Just because a product makes your skin feel or look good immediately after one use does not mean it is *actually* good for you. It's a bit like when you have junk food: it tastes good in the moment, but later can make you feel bad. What I feel is best for my skin is to use what Mother Nature has provided us. I want my skin to be healthy and have a natural glow from deep within, instead of the fake artificial "glow" that's damaging in the long term.

- *Your aura* This is the first thing you'll notice about a person, without even realising. When you feel positive and confident, you're radiating that out in your aura, which will make people feel more drawn to you. The best glow comes from

glowing up

within, so focus on what you're putting in and out of your mind. We have more tips in our next chapter, which is all about mindset.

♥ *Aloe vera* This is one of nature's magical plants. A lot of people know to use it as an after sun, but it also works really nicely as a strong moisturiser. Aloe is full of vitamin C, vitamin E, and beta carotene, which are all amazing for your skin health. We've also tried it as a really natural hair and eyebrow gel. I love how it works because it's quick drying and leaves a slight but dry residue. Just dip a spoolie or toothbrush into it and apply. Make sure you try to get one that's pure and doesn't have any alcohol/chemical preservatives.

♥ *Find your signature scent* How you smell will also leave a subtle but lasting impression on people. One of my favourite things to do is layer my scent. This ensures it lasts all day and is stronger without also being overpowering. What I mean by layering is making sure all the products you use match, like your shampoo, deodorant, moisturiser, and body spray. I really like a vanilla, coconut, or almost salted caramel-y scent, so I like to use things like shea butter as a moisturiser and other products that naturally have that edible scent. Of course, it's fun to mix it up sometimes, too, so make sure to experiment to find out what you like. I also like trying some different floral scents or something muskier and woodier. Remember when I mentioned the skin's good bacteria earlier? It's also

24 grow & glow

super important to consider when using scents, because ingredients like alcohol, which is common in perfumes, are super drying and damaging to your skin's balance. In fact, a lot of perfumes use ingredients derived from petrochemicals, which are made from the same oil that is used to make fuel for cars! In labs, they can use that oil to make almost any scent imaginable, but it's completely fake, of course. These synthetic scents are really hard for the body to detox from, as they're so unnatural. What's great is that now there are

glowing up 25

several brands that use cleaner ingredients. My favourite perfumes are Coconut Sun from The 7 Virtues and Strawberry Letter by Phlur. I really want to try one of the vanilla-scented perfumes from Eden Perfumes too. I mostly use essential oils, though, which are concentrated plant extracts that have the natural smell, flavour, and essence of the source. They can be very powerful, and some do have to be diluted with a carrier oil (like jojoba or coconut), but they are also used to help with a lot of ailments. Lavender and chamomile are great to use if you're feeling anxious and to help you sleep. Eucalyptus is good for clearing out the airways and relieving cold symptoms. Rosemary and peppermint help stimulate hair growth. Tea Tree and Oregano help heal breakouts. I like to use Ylang Ylang and Rose Absolute, which are both floral oils, as perfume because they smell amazing, and you can rub them straight on your wrists and neck.

S   Don't forget Pacifica, Mia! It's a more affordable brand, and their hair & body mists are actually alcohol-free and made using essential oils. They do a lot of other beauty products, too; the highlighters and lip glosses are so pretty.

M

♥   *Neat nails* Making sure the little details like your nails are well cared for makes a massive difference in your overall appearance and as a result will make you feel more put together. Because I love rock climbing (well, what I mostly

26   grow & glow

do is called bouldering), I can't have my nails long or have acrylics, which at first, I was sad about. But to be honest, I feel like natural nails are such a classic and classy look. I kind of like them more this way. I just make sure they're always filed and clean, and sometimes I like to use an organic clear polish, as this makes them look shinier and can help them stay strong. I recently got one that is slightly glittery from a brand called Manicurist, and it's now my favourite look. Lots of nail polishes contain solvents and other chemicals such as triphenyl phosphate, which, from what I've read online, can be harmful when you breathe in the smell, cause skin sensitisation, and affect the nervous system. Some clean brands are Nailberry and the Sally Hansen Good Kind Pure range. I've always loved those nail files that have multiple sides with different types. I feel like the buffer side always makes my nails look so shiny, I don't need any polish anyways!

S I never used to know how to dress or what clothes I liked, until I found my own aesthetic. It can be hard to find something that you feel suits you properly, but it's really worth it, and it's so fun! You don't actually have to stick to one aesthetic. For example, one day I will wear something that's super beach-y and "coconut girl", and the next I will dress tomboy-ish and sporty. I'd recommend finding one main aesthetic that is your style, even if some days you do dress completely differently, as it will help you decide your outfits quicker and know what to buy when you go clothes shopping. Ideally, your clothes should match each other as much as possible,

and it helps if everything has a similar aesthetic. This way, you're less likely to make impulse buys and get something just because it's trendy and then only wear it once. Go for colours that actually suit you and match with each other, and try to only buy something if it actually fits properly so you'll keep wearing it. To help discover what styles you like, do some research, like looking at magazines, Like to Know (LTK app), and Pinterest, and find your favourite individual pieces and overall outfits. You could even make a mood board of the vibe you like. We made this quiz to help you decide:

QUIZ

What aesthetic suits you best

On a day out with your friends, where would you pick to go:
- ✿ Sunbathe at the beach
- ❖ Watch a rock band
- ♥ Have a picnic at a flower garden
- ★ Get a matcha at the mall

What colour would you pick:
- ✿ Bright blue
- ❖ Black
- ♥ Baby pink
- ★ White

Which one word describes you best:
- ✿ Trendy
- ❖ Edgy
- ♥ Girly
- ✿ Organised

What sport would you enjoy the most:
- ✿ Volleyball
- ❖ Skateboarding
- ♥ Ballet
- ★ Gymnastics

Your fave outfits are mostly:
- ✿ Colourful
- ❖ Oversized
- ♥ Cute
- ★ Well-fitting

What kind of jeans do you usually go for:
- ✿ A denim skirt
- ❖ Baggy and in darker washes
- ♥ Ones with cute embroidered details
- ★ A classic strait leg

What's your go-to accessory?
- ✿ Pukka shell bracelet/anklet
- ❖ Choker
- ♥ Bow
- ★ Classic watch

RESULTS

Mostly ✿ You got . . . **COCONUT GIRL**! This style is very Y2K and beach-y. Its iconic motif is the hibiscus flower, and the colour palette is neon but pastel blues, pinks, and yellows. Try adding more pops of colour and some fun tropical graphics to your outfits. Chunky sandals, patterned bikinis, crochet, mermaids, and halter tops are more coconut girl staples. Think California, Barbie, Hello Kitty, and H20: Just add water.

Mostly ❖ Is **GRUNGE**, which is usually a darker and edgier style. It originally came from the rock scene in the 1990s but is also very popular today. Flannel shirts, band tees, slip dresses, bell bottoms, and chokers are the wardrobe staples for the Grunge aesthetic.

Mostly ♥ If you picked this, **COQUETTE** is the style that's most likely to suit you. As with any aesthetic, there's a few different versions of Coquette, but the overriding theme is hyper-feminine. Think frills, pastel colours, bows, and lace. Anything with hearts or cute animals is perfect. If you want to start channelling your inner Coquette girl, try wearing more dresses, anything frilly/puffy, or dainty shoes like pumps.

Mostly ★ **CLEAN GIRL**. This is a trend that became popular on social media, focusing on a natural and effortless look while being very polished and clean looking. The clothing for this aesthetic is timeless, versatile, and well-fitting, with clean lines in a neutral colour pallet. Opt for delicate jewellery, some classic denim, structured blazers, and elegant silhouettes. A big part of this style is the makeup, which is a simple but glow-y natural look. The simpler, the better.

S   I love clothes shopping, but often I end up going home with nothing, or things I don't really like. It's actually really hard to find good clothes because they either don't fit, are too babyish, or are too grown up! I know a lot of tweens and teens have the same struggle as me. I have managed to find some shops I like, so hopefully you'll like these too:

S

- *New Look 915* I love this shop because it's very trendy and has lots of different styles. It also has lots of basics and underwear. They have clothes for ages nine through fifteen at a very good value.

glowing up   31

♥ *Mango Teen* I never really liked Mango's style until I discovered Mango Teen. It's a stand-alone shop with a put-together glam style but still stays on trend. It goes down an extra size than the women's line (although the dresses are still too long for me).

♥ *Urban Outfitters* It has a bit of a thrifting vibe and lots of different on-trend styles. You can find some super-cute dresses here. I would

32   grow & glow

recommend this brand for older teens, but I still love their cute baby tees and sporty outfits. They stock lots of different brands. like Iets Frans, Roxy, Kimchi Blue, and BDG jeans.

M   This is actually one of my faves!

S

- *Subdued* I absolutely love this shop because it's really my style, and as soon as I walk in, I can't leave! They do the cutest tops, super-cool skorts, and the perfect dresses during the summer. I also love their jewellery and accessories.

- *Brandy Melville* They have super-comfy clothes which come in one size. You can wear them out and about and around the house, and some things can even be used as PJs. As I'm writing this, I'm wearing a top and shorts from BM, lol! They also have lots of really nice jewellery, bags, and underwear. It's all in very neutral colours and perfect if you want something that you know will match everything else.

- *Hollister* For cute but still super-comfy dresses, it's the best! They also have a sports store called Gilly Hicks which has some super-cute skorts and floral sports bras. I'd say the style is very American beach vibes.

M   Going into this shop feels a bit like going in a portal to Los Angeles, USA, lol.

glowing up   33

S

- ♥ *Lululemon* Great for sportswear and all sorts of activities. I really love their colourful sets, cropped leggings, and super-comfy sports bras. It's really nice because they go down to a US size 0/UK size 4, and their clothes definitely run small. They are higher end, but it shows in the quality.

- ♥ *Alo Yoga* Also amazing for sporty clothes, I really like Alo because they have lots of items which are so cute, I even wear them when I'm not exercising.

- ♥ *Bershka* They have a very trendy range of clothes, so if you want the latest style, I would definitely look here. They also do lots of tops and dresses for ages ten to twelve, so if you are a tween, then it is a really good place to shop. I like the bags and hats too. (I recently got the cutest pink buckle bag from there).

M One of my favourite hairstyles is twisting the front of my hair back with little clips. I like how versatile it is because you can choose clips to match your outfit, it keeps your hair out of your face, and it works well if your hair is straight, curly, or even a little greasy. I often do this if my hair is looking flat or a day or two after washing.

Y2K Twists

TOOLS: Mini hair clips, tail comb, hairspray, or hair gel.

INSTRUCTIONS:

1. Separate your hair into a middle part and make sure there are no knots.

2. Using the tail comb to make the section neat, grab a small section in a straight line from your scalp. I find it easiest to start from the middle. Twist the hair away from the centre of your head and secure with the clip. Add the hair gel in as you do this if you're using.

3. Repeat until you have a few twists on both sides of your head, trying to make it as even as you can. I usually like to do a total of six. I now spray hairspray to make it secure. My favourite is a natural saltwater hairspray from the brand Rahua. This will help it last all day, but you don't have to use it.

glowing up

S   I love doing bubble braids because it's so quick and really easy. I literally *always* do this style when I have greasy hair or I've got no idea what to do with it.

Bubble Braid

TOOLS: Clear elastics, hair tie, hairbrush, smoothing brush (optional), hair gel (optional)

INSTRUCTIONS:

1. With the hairbrush, pull your hair into a low to mid ponytail, smoothing down any bumps with the smoothing brush.

2. Add a bit of hair gel to the front and sides before securing your hair with a hair tie.

3. Pull the ponytail over one shoulder and put a clear elastic about one to two inches away from your head, depending on how long your hair is.

4. Repeat this, switching which shoulder you put the ponytail over (to make it even and not to one side) until you reach the bottom of your hair.

5. Pull apart each section to make little balls, or "bubbles".

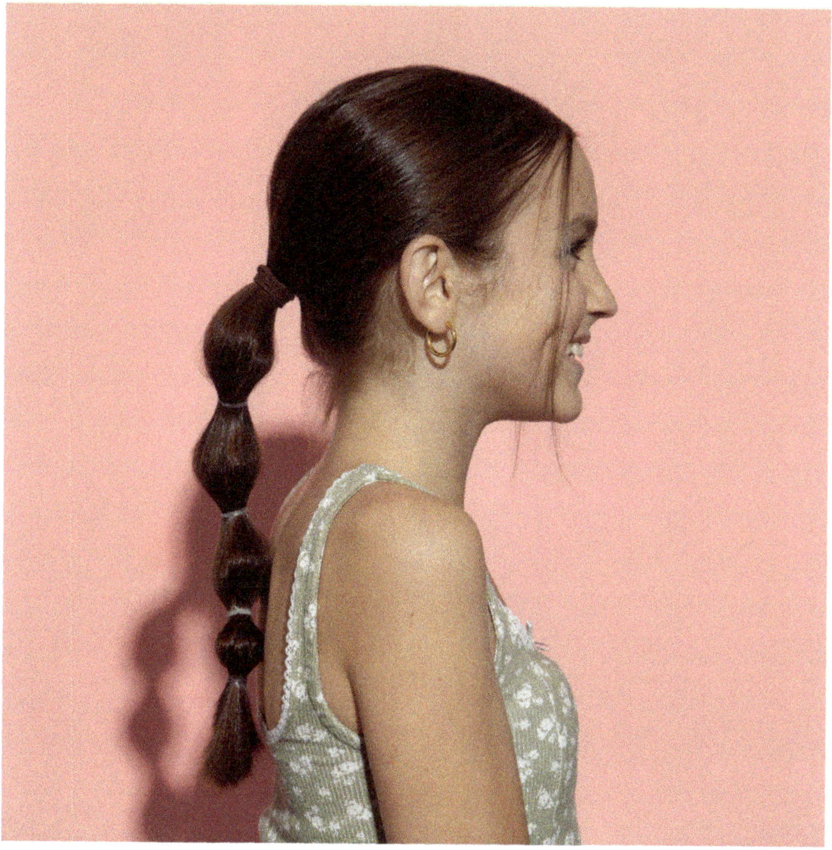

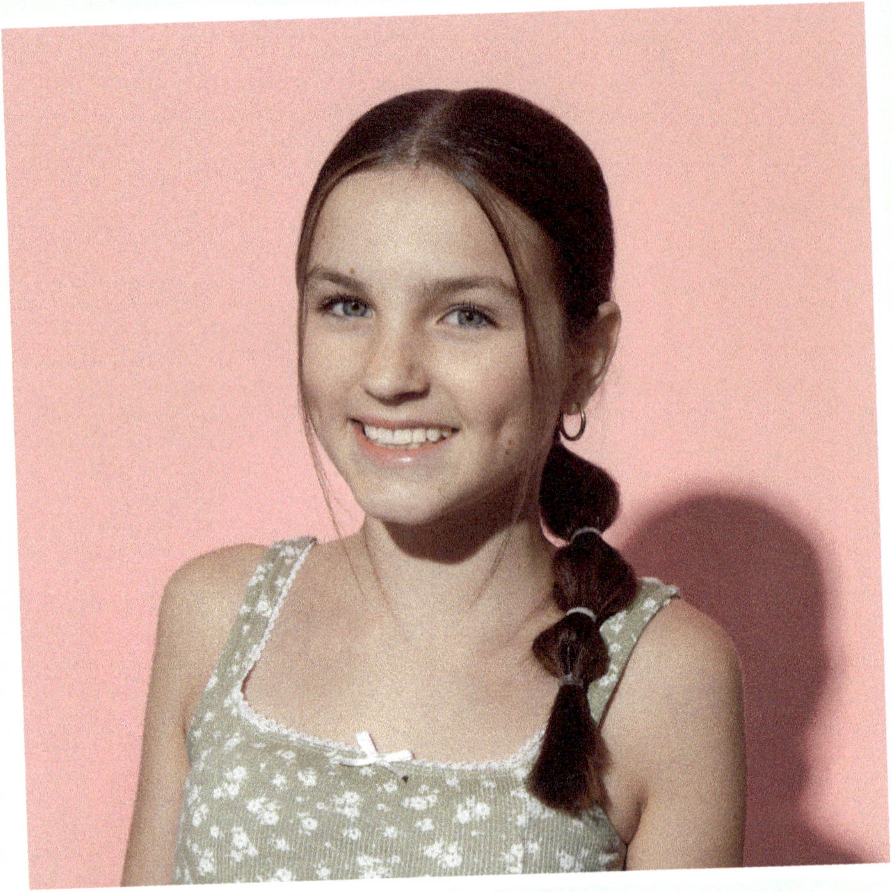

S   How to build the perfect outfit:

- 💗 First you want to have a **comfy but cute top** that fits you really well.

- 💗 **Balance is key**, so if you have a girly top, it can be nice to pick more tomboy bottoms, or if you have baggy bottoms, you probably want a tighter-fitting top.

- 💗 **Jewellery is amazing** because if you have a basic outfit, say a white tee and jeans, but add gold jewellery, it makes it much fancier. Even if you do have a more detailed outfit, jewellery can make it even more complete and put-together. For example, Mia had a really cute outfit the other day, but when she added a crystal necklace, a beaded necklace, and some big hoop earrings, it instantly amped up the outfit and she looked super cool.

M   Aww, thanks, Sienna!

S

- 💗 The same goes with accessories: they can make an outfit a 10/10, or even change the whole style of it! But at the same time, you can overdo it on the jewellery or accessories, so be careful whilst still having fun with it.

glowing up

Challenge

I want you to experiment and wear a completely different outfit or new style to what you normally wear. You could find some old pieces of clothing you don't really wear anymore, or you could ask to borrow something from your friends/sister.

I turned Sienna into my mini-me for the day!

thoughts become things

xoxo

2

One of the scariest things I've ever done was skydiving for my fifteenth birthday. Growing up, I'd always said I really wanted to do something crazy like that but assumed it would have to be when I was way older. Well, while I was living in Dubai, me and my mum went out for brunch with our friend who was visiting. She was telling us about all the tourist-y things she'd been doing, like going to the top of the Burj Khalifa (the world's tallest building), looking around Dubai Mall (which is the world's biggest mall) (don't know if you can notice a theme here, haha), when she told us that she had gone sky diving over the Palm Jumeriah (a collection of artificial islands shaped like a palm tree). I was so excited to hear about her experience, since I'd never met anyone before who had actually done it. I was telling her how much I've always wanted to do it myself when she mentioned she was pretty sure you could do it from thirteen years old in Dubai.

S Actually, the age limit was only twelve. I can't believe I'd be old enough to do it now also. You were SO brave, Mia!

M It was coming up to my fifteenth birthday, and I knew it would be the perfect and most memorable birthday experience, so I begged my mum to let me. She was not keen on it at all, understandably, so I was a bit disappointed but thought I would just have to wait a few more years to be able to make my dream come true. Well, my birthday came around, and guess what my last present was . . . My mum had booked for me to go skydiving the *next* day! I was so unbelievably excited, but it also dawned on me how *terrifying* it was. I arrived at the skydiving centre with my family and met the professional I was going to be strapped to while I was what felt like hundreds of miles up in the sky. He took me through all the safety instructions, and before I knew it, I was boarding the little plane and flying up in the sky. I was so nervous but just trying to think about anything else but what was about to happen. Once we had flown up, the door to the plane was opened, and the couple other people who were also diving started going. It was one of those moments where time goes insanely fast but also incredibly slow. It was finally my turn, and I looked down from the door of the plane and kind of pooped myself, to be honest. Okay, I didn't actually, but I was so high it didn't even seem real. I completely froze up, and my stomach was in my throat, staring down at the ground miles below me. My heart was beating so fast, and I couldn't believe it was actually happening. Luckily, because I was strapped to the professional, I didn't have to snap myself together and make the jump. I was essentially hanging off him with the harness, so he took the leap. The wind was racing and literally blowing my face flat, as you can see in the video on YouTube, lol. It was the most thrilling and exhilarating feeling I've ever felt. When the parachute was released, the whole experience completely changed. Rather than literally falling down straight to the ground, we were now calmly floating. I *loved* it. The view was amazing, and it just felt so peaceful. I'm so jealous of birds because they get to fly in the sky like that every day, so free. When I landed safely, I met my family, and it was so nice to see them again.

Sienna giving me a hug just before I got on the plane.

thoughts become things

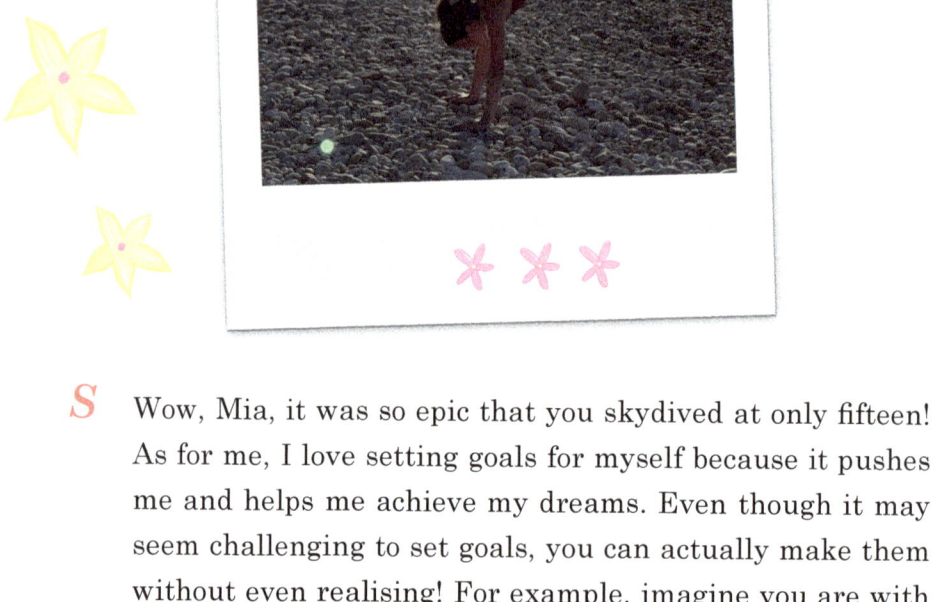

S Wow, Mia, it was so epic that you skydived at only fifteen! As for me, I love setting goals for myself because it pushes me and helps me achieve my dreams. Even though it may seem challenging to set goals, you can actually make them without even realising! For example, imagine you are with your friends at a trampoline park, and they can all do a front flip, but you are not quite able to yet, so you say to yourself, "When I next come to a trampoline park, I want to be able to do a front flip". You, without even realising, have just set a goal. Goals can be about anything, whether you want to have an amazing tan by the end of the summer or you want to learn how to ice skate. In gymnastics, I am constantly setting new goals for myself (for example, I really want to learn a full twist layout on the trampoline and a roundoff back tuck on floor), so if you have a sport you are committed to, then you probably have new goals all the time. And even if you don't do any sports, I've always felt that the same rule applies when setting goals, and that is to start small. The reason for this is so you keep teaching yourself that you are the type of person who achieves your goals, and that then creates a positive feedback loop where you really *do* believe in yourself! So, whatever it is, start small and keep building upwards! You can do it!

Sometimes it can be hard to realise what your goals actually are. I'm quite a creative person, so one of my favourite ways to goal set is by making a vision board, which is a collage of pictures of things you aspire to get or achieve. This is super exciting for me because I get to be crafty. It's also amazing because after I make my vision board, I keep it somewhere I can see it every day, so I'm constantly reminding myself about what my goals are and if I'm actually working on them. To make a vision board, first write a big list of anything you'd like to do in your life. It can be in the next month or in ten years! Don't hold back or wonder if it would actually be achievable—just let your ideas flow. Maybe you want to learn a new gymnastics trick or to crochet; to be able to do a pull up, earn a certain amount of money, buy a designer handbag, or travel to your dream destinations; to have a better relationship with your siblings, a healthy romantic relationship, or more friends; or to run a race, have a certain amount of followers, have waist-length hair, quit wearing makeup, eat healthily every day, or wear a nice outfit every day. It can literally be ANYTHING, the more specific the better. Now get some old magazines and books or, ideally, print out some pictures from online that represent all/any of your goals. You can then decide what goals you feel most inspired by or what's most important to you and lay it all out on a pin board or stick it to a sheet of card. You now have a visual representation of your goals!

S I challenge you to set one goal for yourself and complete it by the end of the week. It could be anything, whether it's not wearing any makeup, waking up and making your bed each morning (to keep your mum happy, haha!), walking one thousand steps, or making £50. When you reach your goal, you should feel really proud of yourself. Best of all, when you have felt the satisfaction of achieving it, believe it or not, it makes you want to set more! M   It might seem like some people are simply born confident, while others are shy, but really the only difference between them is what they choose to be. You might know someone who seems confident all the time, but everyone can feel shy at times and have bad days. That's not to say feeling confident is easy. It's definitely hard and takes work, but it's not impossible for anyone to become more confident. It takes practice. The more you force yourself to get out of your comfort zone, the more it will feel natural for you to do so and for it to become your personality. The more confident you are, the more it will encourage others to be themselves and feel comfortable in social situations. Confidence isn't being a show-off or the loudest in the room. True confidence is being true to yourself and open around others. Someone who's truly confident will make the person they're talking to feel comfortable and uplifted. So how do you begin to feel more confident?

Here are some activities you can do to help you get used to being confident:

- *Compliment people!* I often notice girls wearing a nice outfit or having a good hair day, but it's easy for me to just think it and not say anything. So next time you think it, say it! The worst that can happen is that they don't hear you, but it's way more likely that you'll make their day. I really appreciate it whenever I get a compliment from a stranger, even if it's about something random, like recently a girl at my bouldering gym told me she liked my panda chalk bag, haha.

thoughts become things

♥ *Put yourself in a brand-new social situation*
This can be really scary, but the more you do it, the more you'll believe in yourself. Obviously, sometimes this can happen naturally in life, like when you join a new club or move to a new school. You could also do this by making plans you normally wouldn't, like going to a friend's house or joining in with your grandparent's club. It doesn't matter where you go, it's just the fact of having to talk to new people that will grow your confidence.

♥ *Learn something new* Confidence in something or somewhere comes from experience. Every school I've joined, I might have been a bit nervous and

52 grow & glow

shy at first, but after a while at the school, I became completely relaxed and felt like I could express myself without holding back. What changed? Not the surroundings, but how I felt about my surroundings and the people I was with. Learning a new skill is a great way to teach yourself that you can go into situations with no experience and, after some patience and dedication, become way more confident and comfortable. Both climbing and skateboarding have massively improved my confidence, since I was so inexperienced and had to go through falling over again and again but not quitting. Instead, I stuck at it and became more confident in myself as a result.

S When I was first learning to skateboard, I really wanted to do this skill called a drop-in (where you put the board on the edge of a steep ramp and drop down). It's really difficult and a bit scary, but I kept on trying, and after a couple of months, I could finally do it! I felt so happy, and after a few weeks, I was so confident with it, I could do it barefoot while recording with Mia's phone in my hand. (She was a tad angry with me for that, lol. Sorry, Mia!). Some people saw me and called me the next Tony Hawk (which, btw, is a very famous skateboarder), and it made me feel so confident and encouraged me to learn new and harder skills.

M
♥ *Believe in yourself.* The most important thing if you want to be confident is to believe that you are a confident person. If that seems alien to

you, start by affirming to yourself that you are a confident person and that it is 100 percent possible for you to be so even if you feel like you've always been shy. We don't even have to believe what we're telling ourselves at first! This is more about programming our subconscious, which is the part of our brains that works without us even needing to think about it—like how we can continue breathing whether we think about it or not. So when we repeat positive affirmations to ourselves, it can start to program our subconscious, which in turn affects how we feel. You need to change your belief in yourself by making sure you're telling yourself positive affirmations about how confident you can be and then proving that through your actions by taking risks by putting yourself out there.

♥ *Be inspired by confident people and make that your norm.* As a British girl, I've always been so shocked whenever I've visited America because of how naturally talkative most people are there compared to back home. It's so interesting that something that can seem different for one person is the complete norm to another. But the fun in life is that you can decide what to make your "normal". If you surround yourself with the most confident people you know, and listen to and watch things where people are being more confident, it will slowly become your new normal

thoughts become things

> *"How do you overcome any self-consciousness when vlogging in crowded places?"* BY DEANNA

When I'm with other people, vlogging in public doesn't really bother me. I guess it feels less embarrassing to do something "embarrassing" with others. This just goes to show that nothing is really embarrassing unless you tell yourself it is. There's actually no difference between doing it with others or on your own, except for what you tell yourself. Still, the best way to overcome feelings of embarrassment is not to let yourself overthink it or let those feelings stop you from doing what you want. Remember that you control your own thoughts, so when I feel shy about recording, which definitely happens often, I just remind myself of why I'm filming. I want to make really fun videos for you guys, and often that involves filming outside! The more you do something, the more normal and natural it will become to you, so you can build confidence with repeated exposure. xoxo

thoughts become things 57

becoming a young adult

xoxo

3

The first time I went out by myself was a few years ago. We lived in the countryside at the time, and there was a play park, a local supermarket, a crystal store, and a charity shop near our house. I was super excited, but at first, I was a bit nervous. I had to try to remember the way to the high street because even though I knew the route really well, it felt so different being on my own. I was so used to relying on my parents for directions, but after a while, I became more used to it. Now, I go out by myself often, and it feels normal. It is really important to be aware of road safety and get used to being more street-savvy. I'd recommend asking your parents for advice on being safe while out on your own, and even if they're not comfortable with you going out on your own yet, the sooner you learn, the better. It will also help show them that you are taking it seriously, and with time you can prove to them you're ready.

I've always wanted to be able to drive. It sounds so fun, and it would give me so much freedom to go to wherever I wanted, whenever I wanted. While we lived in Costa Rica, for my seventeenth birthday, my parents surprised me with my very own super-cute pink golf cart. I absolutely loved it and had so much fun getting to drive my friends to the beach. Sienna always used to try to sneak onto the back of it and secretly come with me, haha. It was all great, but my dad always warned me not to drive at night, as there's lower visibility, which makes it more dangerous, especially since the lights on the golf cart aren't that strong. Of course, I didn't listen, because I didn't think anything bad would happen. I didn't fully realise how serious driving actually is. Not to

✽ ✽ ✽

scare you guys off, but it *is* really dangerous if you don't take it seriously and fully concentrate. It's not only your life and your passengers' lives in your hands, but the lives of other people on the road and the surroundings. As you may have seen in our videos, I learnt that lesson the hard way. I wasn't concentrating and was driving at night, so I didn't see the oncoming car when I turned into a junction. It was probably the scariest moment of my life. Since I was obviously only in a golf cart and there were no seat belts, I went flying out the side. I was very lucky that I only hit a small car, and somehow, I only ended up with a few scratches on me, but, oh boy, my golf cart was ruined. I felt so ashamed that I had made such a bad mistake like that, and I definitely should have been taking driving more seriously, but making mistakes is a part of growing up. The main thing is that you actually accept what you did wrong so you can learn from it.

After that bad experience, I thought I'd probably never drive again. I've since realised that because I made that mistake, it can actually help me in learning to drive properly. I now fully understand the seriousness of it. A year later, I started manual driving lessons and took a test in London, but I unfortunately failed. I found driving a manual car really hard and didn't focus enough on it. I was also incredibly nervous and actually vomited before going to my last practise lesson, which was the day before my test. I definitely didn't feel ready when I took it. Despite the fact that all these "bad" experiences make me want to give up, I know how much being able to drive will benefit me. Once I get the hang of it, I know it won't seem like a big deal anymore, so I plan to try again and take another test, but when I'm not living in busy London.

S Money is probably one of the most important things in life nowadays, so it's good to know the basics of it. The best way to learn about money is through first-hand experience by making it for yourself. There are lots of ways, but the easiest ones to start with are bake sales, chores, errands, and selling your art/creations. If you like making cookies, then it would be great to make some and then sell them to your neighbours. (Make sure to save one or two for yourself!) I have made money in lots of ways before, but one of my faves is doing chores for my mum.

Challenge

I want you to get creative and try earning money in a way you never have before!

M   Respecting what your parents want for you when you don't always have the same opinions can be tricky. I think it's a really important part of growing up to discover what you like and dislike by having some freedom to try new things, and inevitably making some mistakes along the way. Of course, no parent wants their child to go through the regret of making a mistake, and it's their job to help guide you and teach you from their own experiences. The best way to work around this is to be understanding and respectful of their decisions, and with time, they will treat you the same way. For example, if you want to get a piercing but are not sure how your parent will feel about it, bring it up to them when they are relaxed and can give you their full attention. Don't demand that you're going to get one, because that will make them feel like they get no say in it. While it is your body, your parents do get a say in choices that can affect the rest of your life, because they have so much more life experience than you and can fully understand the consequences. I'd recommend doing your own research on it first and taking some time to really think it through yourself. Then mention to them how much you like this piercing and why it would really benefit you to get it, if you have their permission, ofc. If they're not keen on it, try to ask them why and really listen to their reasons. Maybe they have done similar things that they now regret or know of others who have. Sometimes, they may not think you're ready for that level of responsibility yet, or don't want you to have to grow up too fast. So, while it is hard, try to remember that it doesn't mean you can never do what you want or have independence. You just have to appreciate the time while you don't have to make bigger decisions and can rely on your parents' judgement for you.

the puberty chapter

xoxo

4

M This story might be a bit TMI, but, hey, puberty isn't exactly pretty, although it is real and completely natural. One evening, I was just casually having a shower when I noticed some red stuff on the floor. I did know about periods, and I knew that I was probably going to start my period soon, as my body had been changing, but I didn't really believe it would happen yet. It was only the tiniest amount, so I kind of convinced myself that I was imagining things, lol. I didn't notice anything else different while getting ready for bed, so I didn't give it any more thought. The next morning, when I used the toilet, I realised that I was definitely not imagining things. I went to my mum and told her that I'd started my periods, and it was definitely a bit hard to open up like that. I found it so embarrassing, and it felt scary to talk about it because it made it more real, but my mum was so supportive, and I'm glad I told her straight away. We went out and had a girly day together and stocked up on some products for me to use.

M Talking about puberty can be so embarrassing, and quite frankly, a bit gross! But it's totally natural, normal, and just a part of growing up. I think the more people talk about it and are educated on what actually happens and why, the better. It can seem really daunting because it's the first time you're going through something like that, but don't worry, every adult understands and knows what it's like.

S For me, puberty is a bit embarrassing, but I don't really feel scared because I have been educated about it. I know it can feel scary for lots of girls, so me and Mia have got our best tips and advice coming up in this chapter. Even though every woman and girl has been through it, is going through it, or will go through it, it can feel like you're the only one, so remember that it happens to everybody!

A lot of different changes can happen to your body and mind during puberty, and this happens because your body is getting ready to become an adult.

It usually happens in this order:

1. Puberty starts in the brain. You'll begin by releasing new hormones which tell the rest of the body to change. Your hormones changing is a big deal and can really affect your mood, motivation, and appetite. I think it's really important to be aware of what might be making you feel a certain way, and to be gentle and take extra care of yourself.

2. The first physical change that happens in both boys and girls is growing pubic hair, but it only starts off as a small amount. Girls also get their first signs of breasts, called a breast bud. It forms under the nipple and can be very tender and itchy. The area around the nipple, which is called the areola, also expands. This usually starts happening around age nine to twelve, but every person is unique and grows at different rates.

3. In the next stage of puberty, you'll go through a big growth spurt and will probably notice that you feel more mature. The breast buds will get bigger, and the pubic hair will get thicker. You'll also notice some hair in your armpits. For girls, your hips and thighs will start to build up more

fat. Boys' voices start to get lower in pitch, and their voice can sometimes "break".

4. At stage four, girl's breast will start to get fuller and are no longer buds. You'll start your periods at this stage, typically at twelve to fourteen. Height growth will start to slow down, but you'll continue to get more and thicker body hair.

5. Stage five is the last part of puberty. This is when your body will have its adult shape, but it can continue to grow a little more. For girls, periods become regular after six to twelve months of having their cycle.

"Why does puberty start late for some?"
BY CHARLOTTE

Just like anything in life, things happen at different rates for different people. It doesn't mean one is better than the other, as, after all, growing up is not a competition. Some people might feel excluded if they're not going through the same things as their friends. My best advice would be to try and not worry: your body knows what it's doing, and there is no rush. Puberty can happen to different people at different rates due to genetics, hormones, or more serious things like illnesses and environmental factors. If you feel like something really different is happening to your body, it's important to try not to panic, as it may be fine, but talk to a trusted adult about it so they can help you if needed.

S During puberty, the sweat glands get larger, so you might become a "stinking ogre" like Shrek, lol (read that part aloud in a Scottish accent). Just joking, but you will need to make sure you keep clean. This can be very embarrassing and a bit gross, so you will probably want to get a deodorant after a while. Make sure to get a natural one because some have harsh chemicals that can be harmful to your body. One of my fave brands is Wild. They do cream ones that come in cute cases with refillable inserts. Definitely shower every day, or even twice if you want, plus after exercise. Try to avoid chemically shower gels and soaps, and instead use natural products. I use a natural shower gel (coconut scented, of course!), while my mum uses a bar of soap, and Mia usually uses just deodorant and makes sure she showers with water enough that sweat never builds up to cause odour.

M What even is a period? Well, it happens once again due to changing hormones, but this time, it's caused by the ovaries, which build up the uterus (or womb) lining so that if there's a fertilised egg, it can attach and develop into a baby. If there is no fertilised egg, the lining breaks down and bleeds out. This process repeats about every month and is the reason why we have periods. It's really magical once you realise that because of periods, you can have children of your own when you're ready. It doesn't mean that having periods isn't hard, though. It can be difficult to manage the bleeding and really affect your emotions and how you feel physically.

Each person's cycle is slightly different, and that's totally normal, but the process is the same and can be broken down into four phases:

1. **Menses phase** The cycle begins on the first day of your period. It's when the lining of the uterus sheds when you're not pregnant. Most of the time this lasts between three and five days. The amount of blood also varies from person to person, but for most it starts off slower, by the second day is the heaviest, and slowly lessens until it's finished.

2. **Follicular phase** This phase overlaps with the menses phase. It begins on the day you get your period and ends when you ovulate (release an egg). During this time, the level of the hormone oestrogen rises and the uterus lining thickens. These changes usually cause you to feel stronger and happier, have more energy, and feel less bloated.

3. **Ovulation** This phase is when your ovary releases an unfertilised egg. It usually happens on day fourteen if the cycle lasts twenty-eight days. During this time, lots of women have tender breasts, and their discharge (fluid which is essential for keeping the female reproductive system clean and free of infection) will change.

4. **Luteal phase** This phase is from day fifteen to twenty-eight. During this phase, if the egg

is fertilised, it attaches to the uterine wall (the inside of your womb), and the woman becomes pregnant. When it's not fertilised, levels of the hormones oestrogen and progesterone drop, and the lining begins to shed, causing the cycle to start over again. Some people notice that the change in hormones causes them to have less energy and more cravings, more swelling and bloating, and breakouts. It really helps to be aware of where you're at during your cycle, if it does affect you, so you can understand why you may be feeling a certain way. I'd recommend tracking your periods on a calendar or app so you can be well-prepared.

M Whether you've already started your periods or not, I think it's a great idea to always be stocked up and have a kit ready. It can be quite fun to make, and I like to add some of my favourite snacks or treat myself to a new lip balm. Then I actually look forward to using my kit! When buying period products, I always try to do some research into the brand and check what dyes etc., they're using. These products are meant for the most intimate area and to be worn for long hours, so when I can, I only like to use organic and pure cotton products. Thankfully, there are so many new brands coming out all the time as more awareness comes to this topic. One of my favourite things are period pants, as they're so comfy for nighttime, it feels just like you're wearing normal underwear. I've made a large kit to keep at home, and Sienna made a mini kit to keep in her bag and take everywhere, since you can never be fully sure when you, or a girl you know, might need some supplies!

the puberty chapter   73

My At-Home Kit

1. Find a large storage box/bag to store all of your supplies in and store it in a cupboard or your bathroom for when you need it.
2. It's nice to have a selection of sanitary products, even if they're not what you typically use, so you always have the option. Some essentials that would be good are panty liners, light- to medium-flow pads, nighttime pads, light- to medium-flow applicator and non-applicator tampons, heavy-flow tampons, period pants, and maybe a menstrual cup.
3. Keep some of your fave healthy snacks here, like dried fruit or raw chocolate.
4. I'd recommend buying some comfy dark-coloured underwear for on and near your period, so you don't have to worry as much if you leak.
5. I love using hot water bottles if I get cramps!

Take-Everywhere Mini Pouch

1. A little bag or pouch big enough to fit everything, but still small enough to put in your bag
2. Your favourite daytime sanitary products
3. Cute lip balm
4. Mini deodorant
5. Mini pack of water wipes/tissues
6. A couple plasters

> *How do you deal with period cramps?*
> BY TYLA

M Cramps are the worst! My best tip: *a hot water bottle.* It's a bit of a family joke that I'm obsessed with hot water bottles, and that's because I really am. I even have a mini one which I take with me whenever I travel. I love it because it's pink and shaped like a pineapple. I feel like hot water bottles are the solution to anything when you're not feeling your best. The heat helps relieve pain, and it feels so cosy. I also like to leave it in my bed while getting unready, so my bed is warm when I go to sleep. I've heard that dark chocolate really helps with cramps, as it's high in magnesium. I like taking warm baths with Epsom salts and calming essential oils, and doing some light exercise, even if it's just going on a walk or doing some yoga, as it will help your body release the "feel-good hormones" endorphins and encourage blood circulation.

M As you start getting boobs, you might want to wear bras. I like wearing them so I feel more comfortable during exercise, or with certain tops, as they help with modesty. You can get many different types of bras, ones with underwire for structure, ones made from tighter fabric to keep your boobs in place, or ones made from soft, malleable fabric for comfort. It all depends on what you're doing and why you want to wear them. It's really important that you get one that fits you properly, especially with underwired or more structured bras. I personally find it uncomfortable to wear bras too often, and I don't think it's very good to wear super-tight and shaped bras a lot. I try to buy clothes that don't need a bra or work with a soft unlined one as much as possible, but it's obviously personal preference.

S I'm actually quite short for my age (I'm thirteen and four foot ten), but I think I've got really big feet for my height (UK size 6), so sometimes I can be very clumsy and trip over a lot. I'll be casually walking up the stairs, suddenly trip, and somehow end up on my butt, haha. Dad always calls out from his office to tell me to stop throwing myself on the floor, lol. This is a normal part of puberty that you go through as you have lots of growth spurts, and it can happen at different rates for everyone. Hormones changing also plays a part in becoming clumsier.

M Everyone gets body hair; it's totally normal and natural. It's definitely not something you should be embarrassed about, but it can be hard to accept when it's new. There are so many ways people like to care for their personal hygiene, but it's absolutely up to you what you prefer. If you do want to remove hair, you could trim, shave, or wax, or there are more permanent hair-removal lasers which you can get done at a professional salon. It's fun to experiment. Just make sure you research and properly know what you're doing. If not, you could injure yourself. I usually shave, as it's quite convenient, but I always make sure I use some natural shaving cream and do it in the shower, so I don't cut myself.

M   Another thing that can happen to some people during puberty is acne. It's super common, and so many people go through it, so try not to stress yourself out about it too much, especially since stress can make it worse! I would recommend looking into your lifestyle to see if there's something that could be causing your acne if you are getting pimples persistently though. I think it's a good idea to use natural products on your skin if you have to use anything at all, and only eat natural foods. I've heard many people say that when they quit processed sugars, oils, and dairy, their skin improved massively. Another factor could be dehydration. I always try to carry a bottle around with me so I remember to drink lots of water—especially if it's hot or I'm exercising! The skin is the biggest organ in the body, so we need to treat it with care and listen if it's giving us signs of an imbalance in the body. Remember that most people won't even notice if you have some "imperfections", and even if it is visible, literally everyone is human and has "flaws" too. When you're older, you won't look back and worry about whether your skin was perfect, but think about how you felt and what you got to experience in life, so don't let something like your skin hold you back.

friendship & crushes

xoxo

When we met the Rybka twins and filmed some super fun YouTube videos together.

5

S My first-ever best friend was when I was six. Because it was so long ago, I don't remember much, except when I first joined my school, she showed me round and helped me settle in. I remember we used to do literally everything together, from eating lunch at break time to going on play dates. She was from Greece, so she always told me about her family that lived there, and it became one of my dream destinations, which was why it was amazing that I finally got to go when I visited Greece just before I turned thirteen. I also remember going to the park together and having so much fun running around and playing tag.

M Throughout our world travels, I've made so many new friends. However, I still tend to feel shy or nervous when I'm meeting people for the first time, but as soon as I get to know them better, I realise that it's no big deal! Making friends if you've moved somewhere new, started a new school, or even if you just want to have more of a social life, can seem impossible at first. My main tip is to be proactive and understand that it will take effort, but it's so worth it, and fun! You can't expect people to just instantly know that you want to be friends, and remember that if you feel shy, it's highly likely that other people do too. Everyone feels shy sometimes!

Here are some ways you could start to make new friends:

- 💗 If you go to school or college, **try to start a conversation with someone new**, especially someone who seems like they want more friends. Invite them to sit with you at lunch or get the bus home together!

- 💗 **Join a club or group for one of your hobbies**, or maybe there's something new you have always wanted to try but not gotten round to. This is great because then you already have common interests, which is a great conversation starter.

- 💗 If you feel like you already know some people but want to get to know them better, **organise a picnic or potluck**! You can even ask people to bring plus ones. This would be a fun way for everyone to meet new people.

QUIZ

What type of friend are you?

What best describes you?
- ✿ Considerate
- ❖ Outgoing
- ♥ Smart

What do you like to do at a sleepover?
- ✿ Bring everyone's fave snacks
- ❖ Play dares
- ♥ Stay up talking

What gift would mean the most to you?
- ✿ You mentioned it once before and they remembered
- ❖ Something that's to do with an inside joke
- ♥ A self-care goodie box

What would you rather?
- ✿ A few friends you've known for a really long time
- ❖ Lots of friends you aren't super close to but have lots of fun with
- ♥ One friend you are super tight knit with and you know everything about each other

What do you do the most?
- ✿ Remember little details
- ❖ Say the best jokes
- ♥ Give good advice

RESULTS

Mostly ✿ You're very **thoughtful**. You love giving gifts and doing kind gestures for your friends. You always try your best to make your friends feel appreciated.

Mostly ❖ You're the **fun** friend. People go to you to have a good time. You always cheer up your friends and aren't scared to be a bit silly.

Mostly ♥ You are super **supportive** of your friends. People go to you for advice, you love long, deep talks, and you're really wise. Sometimes you have to give your honest opinion, even if it is a bit harsh, but you know it will help your friends in the long term.

xoxo

♥ Don't forget to appreciate the friends you do have. The best friendships don't always come when you expect it. It could be your cousin, a family friend, or a neighbour. Putting in a little extra effort and being thoughtful for your friends will definitely be appreciated, especially if it's a friendship you haven't put much effort into before.

If you want to work on your friendships and get to know your friends better, here are some of my ideas:

- ♥ *Get their opinion and advice* It can be for the little things, like what's the best food spot, or bigger, more important things, like something you've been worried about. It could actually be beneficial to you too. If your friends care about you, they definitely want to help you in any way they can. It feels nice to be needed by someone sometimes, so don't be afraid to open up to your friends about any struggles you have.

- ♥ *Organise time to see each other and give full attention* You could gently suggest having phone-free time, like: "Let's go get lunch and catch up! I'm not going to use my phone, as I want to give you my full attention, and I'm so excited to hear everything you have to tell me."

- ♥ *Ask them about their goals and dreams*
  You may know everyday things about your friend, but do you actually know them below the surface? You might be surprised by what you learn about them if you take the time to ask.

S Here are some questions I think would be fun to ask:

What's the best memory of us that you have?
What's your spirit animal?
What's the weirdest dream you've ever had?
Do you have a celeb crush? If so, who?
*What's one song you always play
to make yourself feel better?*

M Sometimes it's easy to get caught up in the moment and accidentally say things you don't really mean. This has definitely happened to me before, and I know I've hurt someone's feelings as a result. The main thing is that you take full accountability that you made a mistake if you do upset someone, properly apologise, and don't push away any feelings of shame but really accept that you made a mistake so you can learn to be more conscientious in the future. Of course, not everyone will have the same opinions or humour as you, so a natural part of life is that sometimes you might offend people by accident, but if you think what you're about to say might hurt someone, pause and consider if it's actually helpful and necessary for you to say it. For example, if you see someone walking around with toilet paper on their shoe, it would actually be helpful to politely let the person know, as they probably don't realise and can easily remove it there and then. However, that doesn't mean if you see someone wearing something you dislike, you're entitled to tell them your opinion. That person clearly knew what they were wearing when they got dressed and chose it because they wanted to, so for you to say something negative isn't helpful at all. Of course, if someone asks for your opinion, that's a different story, but there are still ways to word it tactfully. Always try to put yourself in the other person's shoes and consider how it would make you feel if someone said that to you.

friendship & crushes 87

S   My first crush was when I was nine and we were living in Costa Rica. Me and Mia used to go to the basketball court where all the kids in our community went to hang out, and the boys took the casual matches way too seriously, lol. I was the youngest of all the kids, as most of them were teenagers, but there was this one boy who looked a lot younger than he actually was. Because of this, he sometimes got teased that he had a crush on me. The problem was that he had absolutely no interest in even being friends with me because I was three years younger than him, but I really wanted him to notice me. I remember one time he had some Tic Tacs, and he gave some to his friends, and then offered one to me! This was probably the first time he had properly ever spoken to me, so I was very excited. He was into skateboarding and surfing, which was exactly what I liked at that time too! I also did a lot of biking then, and the most embarrassing thing happened to me. I was dropping off some old toys at a friend's house, and I was a bit off balance because of the big bag I'd hung on one handlebar of my bike. On the way to my friends, I passed the basketball court, and my crush just so happened to be there. Just as I went down a little but steep slope, he scored a goal, and I looked over at him to see what the cheering was about, and I started wobbling so much that by the time I got to the bottom, I was completely out of control. My bike went to the side because of the bag, and I fell to the ground, hard! It really scared me, and my knee was bleeding, but the worst part was that my crush saw it all.

M   Omg, Sienna, that's so embarrassing!

S   I know, I just wanted to disappear into the ground! He called down to check if I was okay, so I mumbled yes, and, feeling very embarrassed, I got on my bike and biked away as fast as I could. I was not badly hurt, but I was so embarrassed when I played basketball with everyone later that afternoon.

M I used to think peer pressure was something that only happens when you're young, but it actually can happen at all ages. If you're not sure about something, don't let other people talk you into changing your mind about it. Think about how you're going to feel about yourself after, and if you're not sure, it's best you go with your initial opinion. Of course, sometimes friends can encourage you to do good things, and that's great,

friendship & crushes 89

so peer pressure isn't just negative. This is exactly why it's really important to realize that if someone's encouraging you to do things you don't feel good about, they're not really a true friend. If you say no once, you shouldn't have to repeat yourself. If someone doesn't take that as your answer, they're not a true friend who really cares about you. If you're surrounding yourself with friends who are into the same things as you and are making positive choices in their life, that will encourage you to do the same, and it's the kinder option for both you and others. If there's someone you've known for a while who's changed, it can be hard to see, but hopefully with your example, you can inspire them to make more good choices too. Sometimes that might mean that you'll have to distance yourself a bit. If they really care about you and want to make better choices, this will hopefully make them realise they need to make some changes, and if it doesn't, it shows that maybe they're not really worth your time anyway

" *How do you deal with breakups?* " BY CHARLIE

Going through a breakup can be really hard, so be gentle on yourself. There's no rush to force yourself to feel back to normal, as pushing away your feelings can be unhealthy in the long term. You just need to focus on taking care of yourself and trying to do things that make you happy. The busier you keep yourself, the better. Remember that you had a life before this person, and you can definitely have a really good life after. This doesn't mean that what you had with them in the moment wasn't special. Sometimes things just aren't meant to be forever.

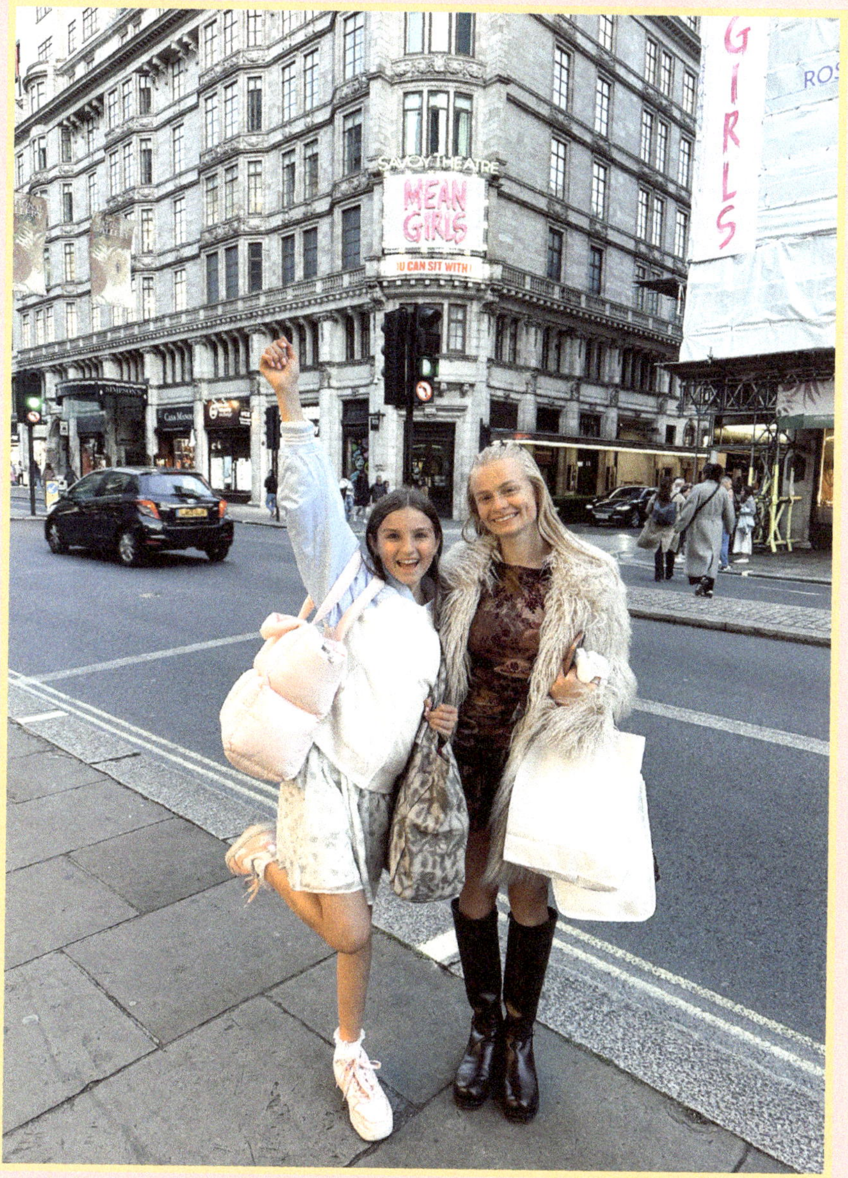
SAVOY THEATRE
MEAN GIRLS
GIRLS

eat to glow

xoxo

6

You might not know this about me, but I've actually been vegan my whole life! My parents decided to go vegan when I was born, so I don't really know what it's like being any other way. I really love being vegan, though, because I don't think it's fair for animals to suffer just for me to have specific foods, when I can easily eat the vegan version. I know for some people it can sound hard or even scary to give up their "normal" food for vegan options, but I've heard a lot of non-vegan people saying the vegan substitute tastes the same or even better! Although it is best for our health to eat natural foods the way nature made them, there are still so many vegan options that aren't just lettuce, so if that's what you're thinking, don't worry: you can get vegan versions of everything from burgers to pizzas, milkshakes, ice cream, and more. But remember, just because it's vegan, it doesn't necessarily mean it's healthy. Some people might eat a balanced diet, but when they decide to go vegan, they start eating loads of processed food just because it has a vegan label. In this situation (although it's obviously not kind to the animals), it would be healthier to eat a balanced non-vegan diet than a vegan one full of junk food. With that being said, you can still eat some treats now and then, as long as you try to eat predominantly healthily. I like a roughly 90 percent healthy and 10 percent occasional treats ratio so I feel strong and healthy yet still get to enjoy some indulgences too! Eating organic when you can is also really important because most vegetables are sprayed with harmful chemicals to kill the bugs, and to be honest, if they can kill insects then they are probably not too good for us either, lol. We go to a local farmers market to buy most of our organic vegetables, but almost all supermarkets have an organic fruit and veg section also.

I am the biggest foodie. I LOVE my food. I especially love food that tastes amazing in the moment as well as makes my mind and body feel good after eating. The way I view it, food is building blocks for the body. You are literally made from what you eat! If you're used to eating mostly junk foods, it can be hard at first to start eating healthier. But the main thing is that you try your best. It's better for you to eat some fruit with something unhealthy than none at all. In fact, fresh fruits and vegetables can actually help negate any of the bad effects of less healthy foods. The more healthy foods you eat, the more you'll notice how you feel from junk foods, and the less you'll want to eat them. It's literally science, since your gut bacteria actually sends signals to your brain as to what to crave. The more you eat something, the more of the bacteria that like that food will proliferate and tell your brain to eat more of it! As you can imagine, it quickly becomes a cycle, so if you're not happy with your current diet, all it takes is to start breaking out of that cycle. How do you do that though? It can seem overwhelming at first. But really, it's quite simple! It's all about the little choices you make in your day-to-day life. You definitely shouldn't go without, as that's not healthy and won't last as you'll feel lack, but instead make some simple switches.

Did you know?

Most chewing gum is actually made out of plastic! This means that every time you have gum, you're actually chewing on plastic, and little micro bits can even go into your digestive system. Luckily, there are lots of brands that are made from natural ingredients nowadays, and they work the same. I must admit that some brands are better than others, so try a few out to find your fave.

Here are some healthy switch ideas to get started:

💗 *Candy to dried mango* **Mango** is one of my fave fruits, especially dried, because, like a lot of candy, it has that sweet and slightly sour kick. It's so morish! I also think dried pineapple works really well as an alternative. The processed sugar that is in candy is really hard for the body to deal with and also incredibly addictive, so it's best to avoid it as much as possible. The naturally occurring sugars in fruit taste just as good, and drying the fruit accentuates the flavours and makes it easy to take everywhere with you.

💗 *Ice cream sundae to acai bowl* Acai is a berry that comes from Brazil, but it's quickly becoming super popular all round the world. When I'm craving a sweet but cold treat, I love going to an acai spot where they serve frozen acai blended into an ice cream-like consistency and usually have lots of different toppings you can choose from. It's super delicious, and just as fun, I love having nut butter and fresh fruit on top.

- *Soda to sparkling water with fruit* It's easy to forget that drinks that aren't just water can actually have a lot of unnatural ingredients (especially processed sugar). It's really important to drink as much pure water as you can so your body is properly hydrated, but obviously it is nice to have a flavourful drink sometimes. There are a lot of healthy drink brands out there nowadays which use sparkling spring water as a base and then flavour it with a touch of fruit, or you could make your own at home. It's super easy: just add some freshly cut fruit (or you could try freeze-dried) to still or sparkling water.

- *Chips to baked sweet potato wedges* I always prefer baked over fried because when oil is heated to really high temperatures, it can make it much harder for the body to digest. I've always been a fan of sweet potatoes since I was a little baby. They're bright orange inside, full of vitamin A, and slightly sweet (hence the name). I think they're better than your average potato because they have way more nutrients, and I prefer the flavour!

eat to glow

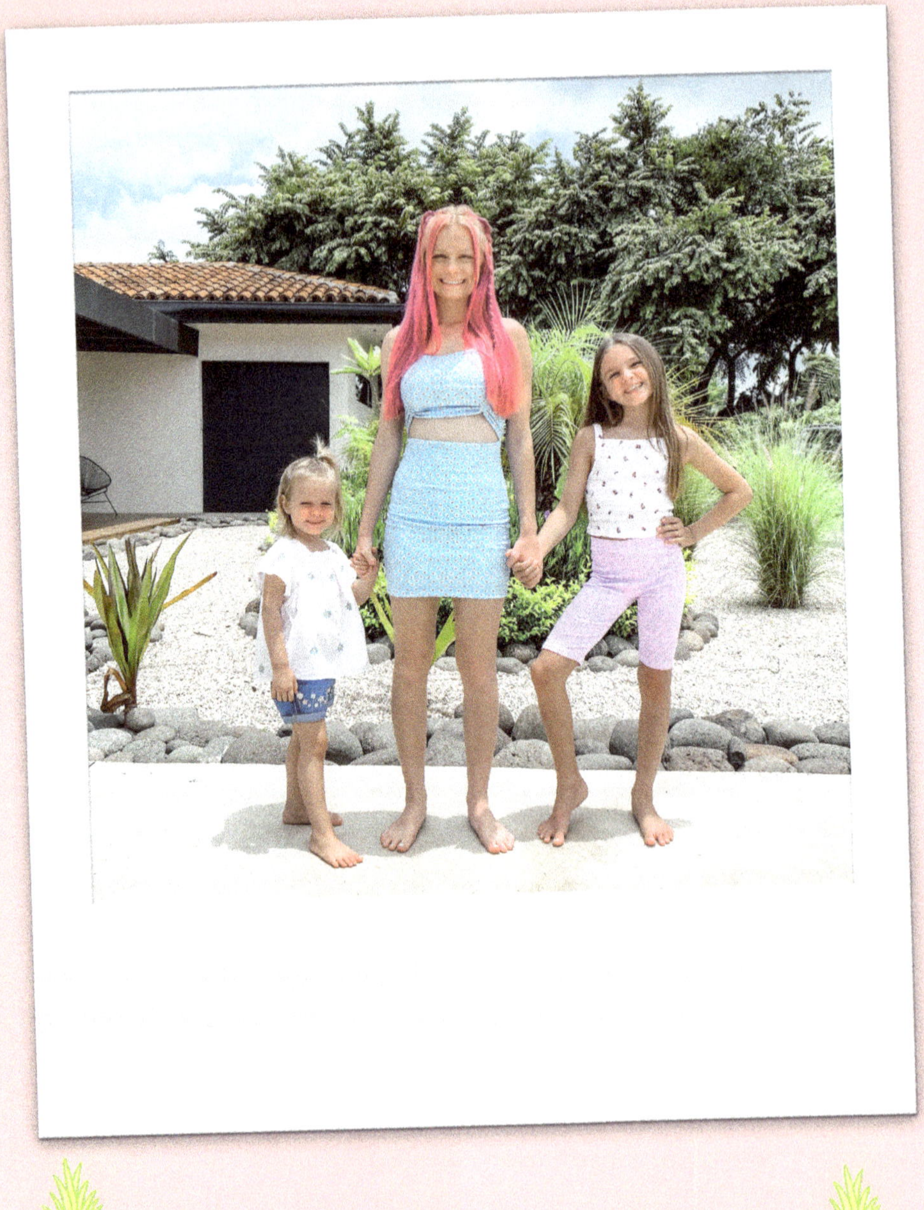

S Top tip

When you want to have a fizzy drink, first have a
glass of water. Then if you still want the drink, have it.
This way you're getting proper hydration first and know you're
not just having the fizzy drink to quench the thirst. It's also
a good way to wean yourself off sugary drinks.

RECIPE

Vanilla and Strawberry Smoothie Bowl

This is one of my fave things to have as breakfast, as it doesn't feel too heavy to digest but is still super satisfying and gives me enough energy to start my day. You can, of course, adjust the measurements based on how hungry you are. This recipe is so creamy yet sweet and feels really nostalgic to me as it reminds me of picking strawberries when I was a kid. You can use other fruit, but I would recommend that it's frozen, as it helps the bowl to be a thicker consistency. Go as crazy with the toppings as you like. I love experimenting with different textured foods, like granola, as the crunch really adds to it. It only takes like five minutes to make too!

Ingredients
- 1 cup non-dairy milk (My fave is soya.)
- 1 medium to large banana
- ⅓ cup oats
- 1 scoop vanilla protein powder (optional)
- 2 large handfuls of frozen strawberries

Toppings: granola, any fresh fruit, desiccated coconut, chocolate

Instructions
- Place all the ingredients into the blender. I recommend starting with the soft/wet ingredients first to help it all blend.
- Blend on high speed until there are no clumps.
- Pour into bowl and add your desired toppings.

S RECIPE

Sienna's Avo on Toast

This is the BEST lunch ever. I always make this because it's super easy, and it only takes 5 minutes maximum. You can make it plain or add the extra toppings. The avocado is really creamy, while the toast is crunchy, so it makes the perfect combo.

Ingredients

2 slices of sourdough bread

1 avocado

Olive oil

Sea salt

Pepper

Extras: Cress or other sprouts, sauerkraut/kimchi, chopped tomatoes, squeezed lemon.

Instructions

- Slice the bread (I like it thick, but you can make it however you want) and put it in the toaster.
- While the bread is toasting, cut the avocado in half and throw away the stone.
- When the toast is ready (just how you like it), use a spoon to scoop the avocado onto the toast, and then use a fork to mash it all up.
- Add the salt, pepper, olive oil, and optional extra toppings.
- Enjoy!

M RECIPE

Poke Bowl

I love this bowl because it's pretty simple to make and is so versatile but still feels like a proper meal. All you have to do is prepare some rice, then top with whatever you fancy. There really isn't anything more to it! I use sticky rice, as it's more authentic and I like the texture, and I cook it in my pressure cooker, which makes it even more simple. There should be instructions on the back of the rice packet too. While the rice is cooking, I chop and prepare my toppings. You can go for more Asian-inspired ones like I have, or just use whatever fresh things you have in your kitchen. Don't forget to add some soy sauce, mayo, sriracha, or any other sauce, as they really complete it. It took me about fifteen minutes to prepare this, and there was minimal washing up.

Mia's fave toppings
Tempeh/tofu
Sweetcorn
Sweet potato
Diced chilli
Flaked seaweed
Soy sauce
Mayo

Sienna's fave toppings
Edamame
Nut-based cheese chunks
Cucumber
Avocado
Mango

S RECIPE

Sienna's Chocolate Brownies

I love these brownies because they are the perfect snack and dessert and are great for picnics! The cornstarch and water mix actually make something called *ooblek*. It's a mixture that is not a solid and not a liquid, so it's super interesting, and every time I make this recipe, I get a bit carried away playing with it! These brownies taste really rich and sweet while being super gooey.

Ingredients

- 1 ½ teaspoon cornstarch
- 1 teaspoon water
- ½ cup melted coconut oil
- 1 ½ cups coconut sugar (You can use brown, but coconut is the healthiest.)
- ½ cup soya milk (or another type of non-dairy milk)
- 1 teaspoon vanilla extract
- 1 cup gluten-free plain white flour
- ½ cup unsweetened cocoa powder
- 1 teaspoon baking powder
- 1 pinch of sea salt
- 2 handfuls of chocolate buttons/chips

Instructions

- Turn oven to 180°C.
- Get a big bowl, add the cornstarch and water, and mix thoroughly until it makes the "ooblek".
- Now add all the other wet ingredients to the bowl and whisk together. It should have a thick syrup consistency.
- Sift the flour and cocoa powder into the wet mixture.
- Add in baking powder and salt, then mix until the batter turns gooey. This is a good time to give it a little chef taste.
- Mix in the chocolate buttons. (Make sure they are mixed thoroughly. If not, some slices will have too many, while some will have none). You could also add nuts or fruit.
- Pour the batter into a greased 8-inch tray.
- Bake in the oven for 30 minutes, until the outside is crusty. It's okay if the inside is still a little gooey, but it shouldn't be like batter anymore.

Mia's Chocolate-Coated Caramel Dates

Sienna's Chocolate Brownies

RECIPE

Mia's Chocolate-Coated Caramel Dates

These are so simple to make and are made from **only four** healthy ingredients. You're really going to struggle to believe it once you try them. They're the perfect combo of sweet, slightly salty, and rich, so I can guarantee these are going to be your new addiction. I like these as a quick dessert or ultra-decadent snack. The crunchy-ness from the chocolate works perfectly with the gooeyness of the date. It's just like a candy bar, but even **better**. And it should only take five minutes for you to make and ten minutes in the freezer!

Ingredients
- 1 pack of dates (or as many as you want to make)
- 1 bar of organic chocolate (I used one made from coconut sugar, as it's the healthiest.)
- Nut butter (My fave is almond.)
- Sea salt

Instructions
- ♥ Break up your chocolate and place it into a small bowl. Fill a smaller saucepan with boiling water on the hob, then place your bowl over it. You want it to be big enough so it doesn't fall into the water and just slowly melts the chocolate with heat from the steam.
- ♥ Slice into your dates so you can remove the pits, but don't cut enough for them to break in half. Remember to keep slowly stirring the chocolate and be careful not to get it too hot, or it will burn.
- ♥ Fill each date with a spoonful of nut butter and sprinkle of salt and try to re-close.
- ♥ Now, you can either half dip or roll one date at a time into the melted chocolate so they're fully coated. Place on a plate in the freezer for ten minutes, or until the chocolate is hard.
- ♥ Store them in the fridge and enjoy when you're craving a sweet bite!

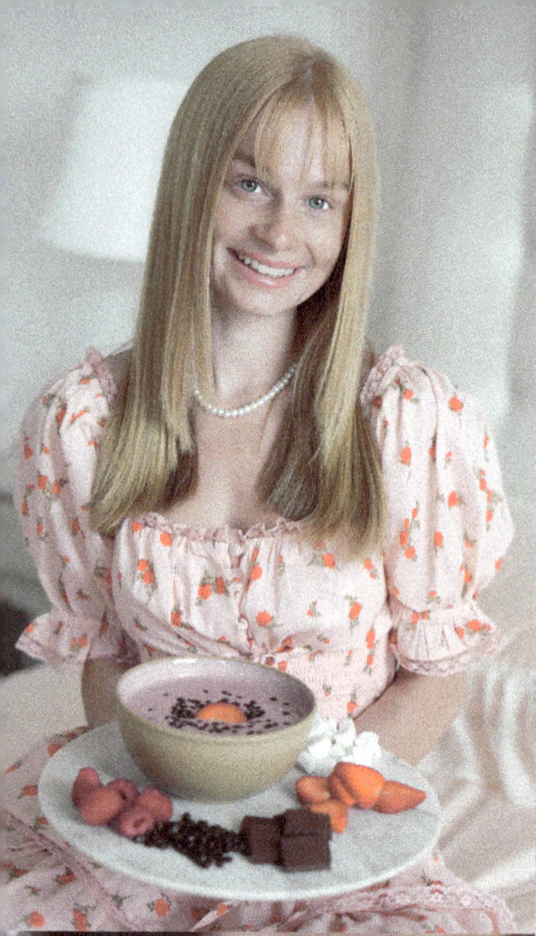

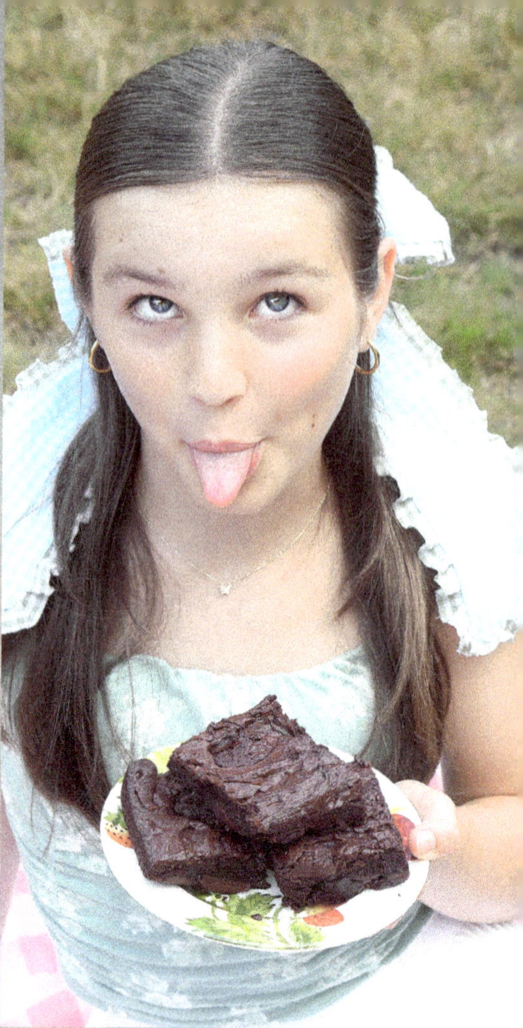

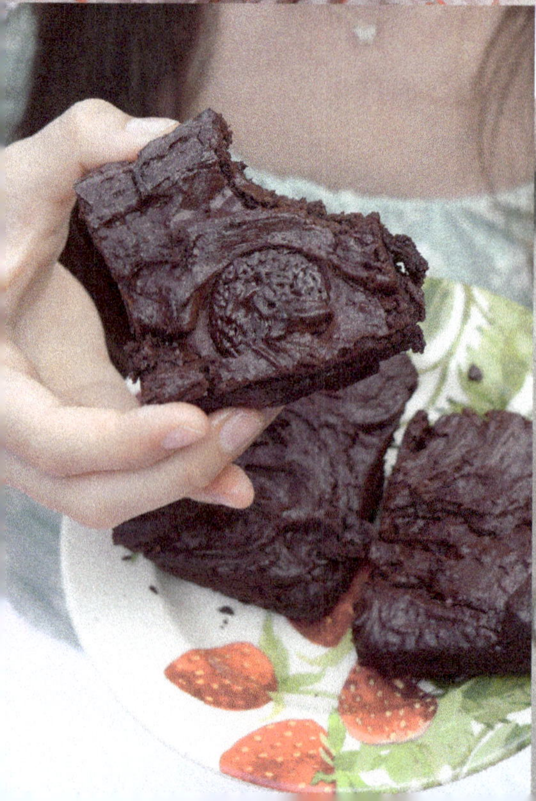

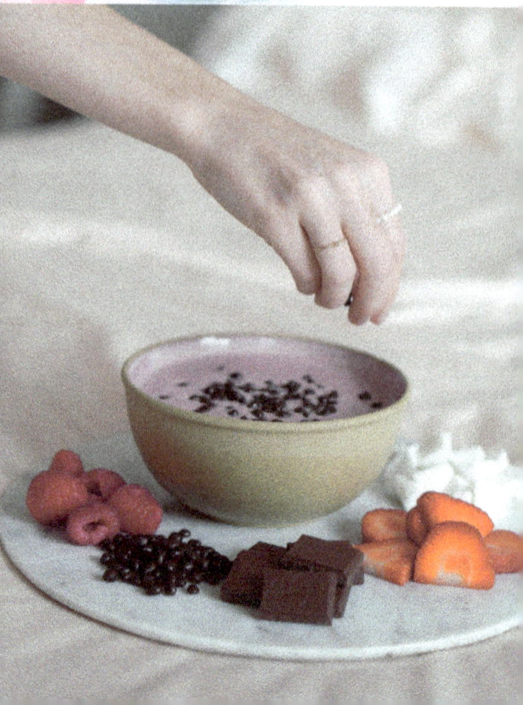

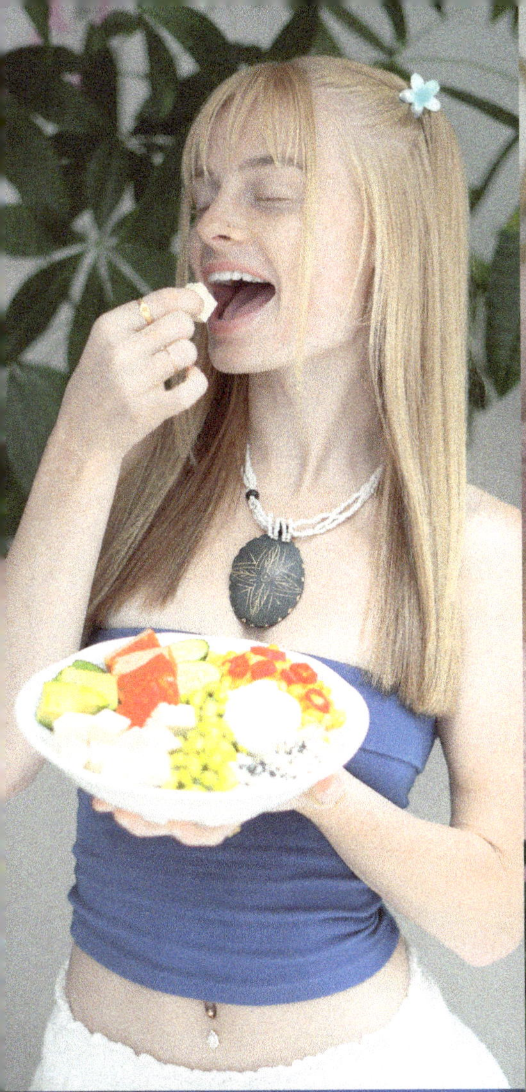
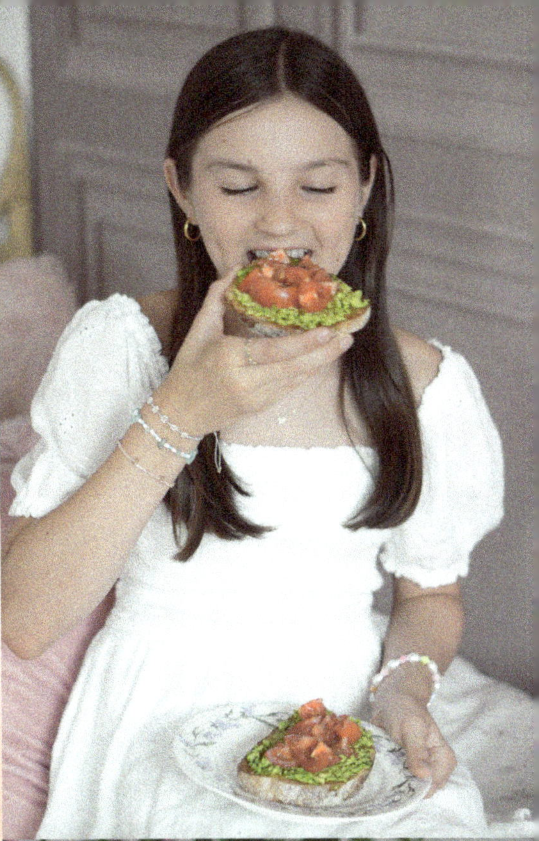
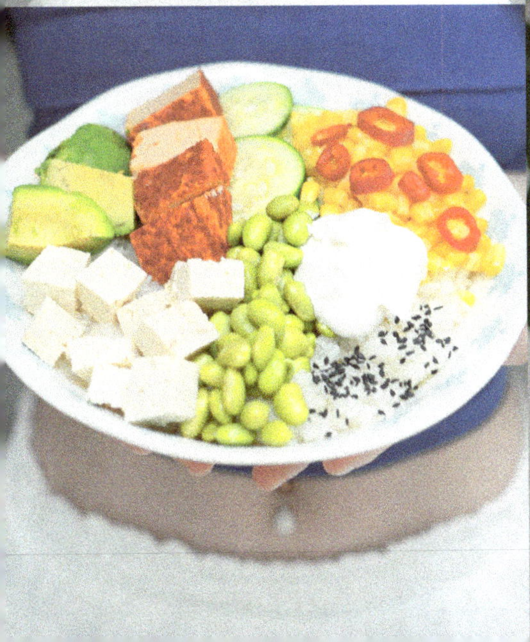
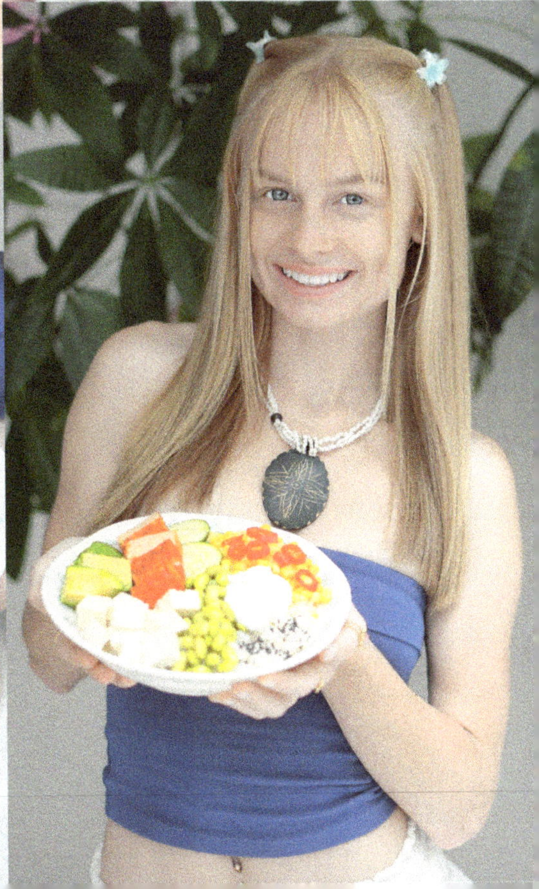

all about family

xoxo

7

S I've got so many hilarious stories that involve my family, but this one is probably my fave. First of all, I want to say sorry to Mia for exposing her, lol. So, when I was about six or seven, me and Mia were on holiday in Los Angeles, California, and Mum and Dad had left us home alone, happily playing Monopoly. We were playing for about an hour when Mia looked up and said, "What is that on the wall?" There was brown liquid running down the living room wall! We both immediately ran upstairs to see where it was coming from, and when Mia looked in her bathroom, it was flooded with the same brown water coming from her overflowing toilet. She had accidentally blocked her toilet and not realised until it was too late! We (or more like just Mia) then tried to clean the house before Mum and Dad came back, but they still saw the giant mess and were not very happy about cleaning dirty toilet water off the walls of the house we were staying in. Thankfully, we managed to clean the whole house so well that the house owners never noticed (or at least they didn't say anything). Now I think Mia always makes sure not to block the toilet, haha.

M In my book *Awkward to Awesome*, I actually interviewed Sienna, who was only seven at the time, and it was hilarious. I thought it would be really funny to interview Karma as a throwback to that, plus I wanted to find out how she *really* feels about us. Us holding baby Karma.

Interview with Karma

Sienna Hey, Karma, welcome to our interview!

Karma Hi!

Mia OK, for the first question: What's your fave thing to do ever?

Karma Probably going to the park.

Mia Aww, why do you like the park?

Karma Because I like playing in the sand.

Mia That's so cute.

Sienna The next question is about Koa. What do you like most about having a brother?

Karma When he kisses me before bed.

Mia Aw, that's so sweet. What do you like the least about having a brother?

Karma He's annoying because he always steals my stuff and breaks it.

all laugh

Sienna Yeah, he does that to me, too, sometimes. What do you think you would prefer, eating a whole chocolate cake or a whole pizza?

Karma A chocolate cake!

Sienna Really, a whole chocolate cake? But don't you think you'd feel sick?

Karma No. *shakes head enthusiastically*

Mia But why the chocolate cake over pizza?

Karma Because I like it and . . . pizza is gross.

Mia What? Really?

Karma Yeah!

Sienna If Mia was a colour, which one would she be?

Mia Oooh, I hope you pick a nice one!

Karma Uhm . . . blue.

Mia Blue, why?

Karma Because blue is the colour of the sky and my second favourite colour.

Mia Hmm, that's interesting. What about if Sienna was a . . . flower. What would she be?

Karma A flower? Uhm, a dandelion.

Sienna A dandelion! Why a dandelion?

Karma Because they're pretty.

Sienna Aww, thanks, Karma. But they're also weeds that dogs wee on tho.

Karma laughs

Mia Well, hopefully no dogs use you to wee on. Anyways, Karma, what do you like most about doing gymnastics?

Karma I liked when we did gymnastics in Spain. We went in the foam pit, and I got to do front flips into it.

Mia Oooh, I bet that was fun. What's your best gymnastics trick then?

Karma Uhm, a cartwheel.

Sienna You can also do a roundoff! That's harder.

Mia Yeah, you're really good at both of those.

Karma Well, they're kind of the same. And I can do a backbend down a wall!

Sienna If you could be any age, what would you be?

Karma A million! Then I could do anything I wanted.

Everyone laughs

Mia What's your fave hobby?

Karma Doing arts and crafts.

Sienna What kind of things do you make?

Karma I do pictures in my notebook. I like drawing the beach.

Mia Aww, thanks for being in our interview, Karma!

Sienna Yeah, thanks, Karma! This was so fun.

Karma You're welcome.

S Most of my favourite memories are with my family. Although siblings can be annoying and parents can be controlling, you have to remember that they really love you. Sometimes it can be a bit annoying to have a little minion following you around, but at the same time it's also really fun being a big sister. Having an older sibling being bossy or not letting you hang out with them can sometimes suck, too, but you will always have someone to ask for advice, learn from, and talk to. I am really lucky because I get the experience of being a little sister and a big sister. Technically, I'm a middle child, but I think that expression downplays being in "the best of both worlds". If you're an older sibling, then try to remember your younger siblings just want to be like you, and although this is easier said than done, try to set a good example. If you are a younger sibling, then make sure to respect your older siblings and their personal space. If you are being annoying, then they are probably NOT going to let you go shopping with them.

Look how cute baby Karma was at this family photoshoot.

all about family **113**

M Growing up, it can be easy to forget that this is also your parents' first time at life. Yes, they have a lot more life experience than you do, so it's important to respect them and the fact that their role in your life is to look after you and make sure you can be the best version of yourself. You might not always agree, or it might feel like they're trying to stop you from doing the things you want, but parents ultimately want their children to be happy. I know it can be hard in the moment, but try to be understanding to your parents. There is no guidebook that comes with being an adult or parent, they're just trying their best with their own life experience.

If you want to strengthen a relationship, the best way is to put effort in and be thoughtful to the other person. Make room in your calendar for quality time with them, remember to give them thoughtful gifts (it doesn't have to be big, could just be their favourite chocolate), or do little favours for them. Plan some day trips or activities to do with them.

Here are some which I'd love:

- ### Go to the park or beach and have a picnic
  This is such a fun and relaxing activity. It's really important for your mind and body to get out in nature as much as you can, so why not encourage your loved ones to come too.

- ### Make a meal or bake with them
  Food always tastes better when it's made with love and eaten with others! You can make something quick and simple or be adventurous and follow a completely new recipe.

- ### Offer to help them with the little things
  Maybe they need some things from the shop or their car/wardrobe needs cleaning, or you could make them breakfast so they have more time in the morning. Especially if it's something you're going to be doing anyways for yourself, if you just take that little extra time to consider them, they'll definitely appreciate it.

♥ **Make a goodie box for them** You can put in their fave snacks or even a lip-gloss/perfume. I know this would really make my day.

♥ **Go to a photo booth together!** This is such a cute activity to do, and you can look back at the photos you got together.

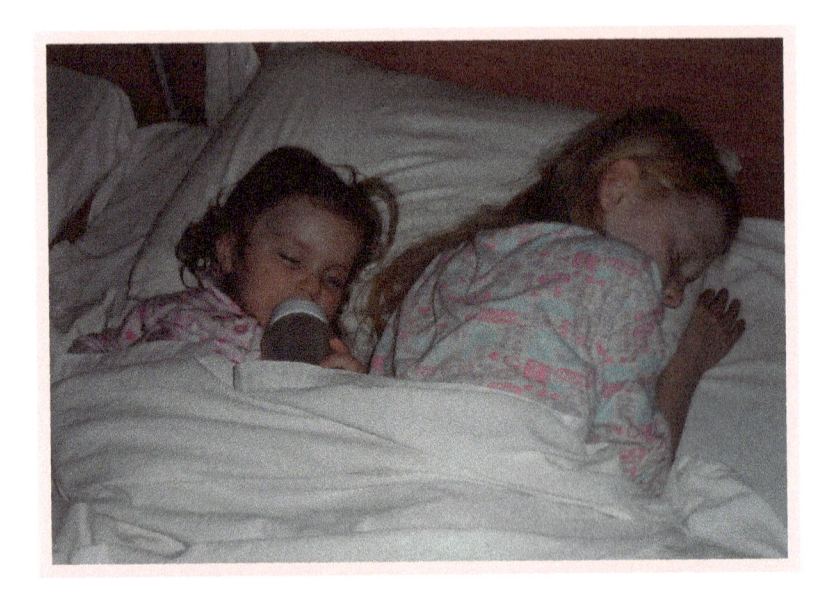

S I really love spending time with my grandparents, because they always have the best stories to tell about their childhood. My great-grandma told me she used to pick up my grandad from school wearing tiny hot pants! Grandparents can also be very wise, as they have been alive through the decades. Next time you see your grandparents, why not ask them about their life as a teen? Make sure to appreciate spending time with them, as they won't always be around, and they can actually be super fun to hang out with.

While spending quality time with your family is really important, especially if you want to be closer with them, making sure that you have personal time will help too. If you're constantly stepping on each other's toes, literally and figuratively, you're not going to appreciate the time you do spend with them as much. Sometimes distance can make bonds even stronger. As the saying goes, "Distance makes the heart fonder". Here are some ways to make personal time for yourself:

- If you share a room, **make a rota** with set times for you to use the room alone for things that you want more privacy for, like studying, practicing an instrument, working out, reading, or filming a video.

- **Create your own space** Find a spot in your house that you can decorate however you like. It could be an area in the garden, your bedroom, or even a windowsill. Keep your favourite books, whatever makes you feel comforted, or what you enjoy doing here. Maybe hide some snacks, haha! It would also be nice to decorate it according to your aesthetic; it could be simple things like a candle, some artwork, a cushion, or some flowers.

- **Get out!** Instead of constantly shouting that at your siblings, haha, try to put in the extra effort to do some things out of the house that you normally wouldn't. I always really enjoy going to the park when I paint, but you could get on with some computer work at the library/cafe, take breakfast with you and eat it outside, or just

all about family

go for a little walk/jog. This really helps me feel refreshed and clears my head, especially if I've been super busy or I'm overthinking.

> **What advice would you give your younger siblings when they grow up?** BY LULU

M To make the most of every moment you have at the age you are now and not wish away time to be older. I know it's something that every adult says, but it is *so* true. I feel like it's one of those things that you might have to learn by growing up and going through it yourself though. But, yeah, my biggest advice would be to remember there is no rush to do anything right now. Life moves quickly, and before you know it, you'll be able to do all the things you want to do. xoxo

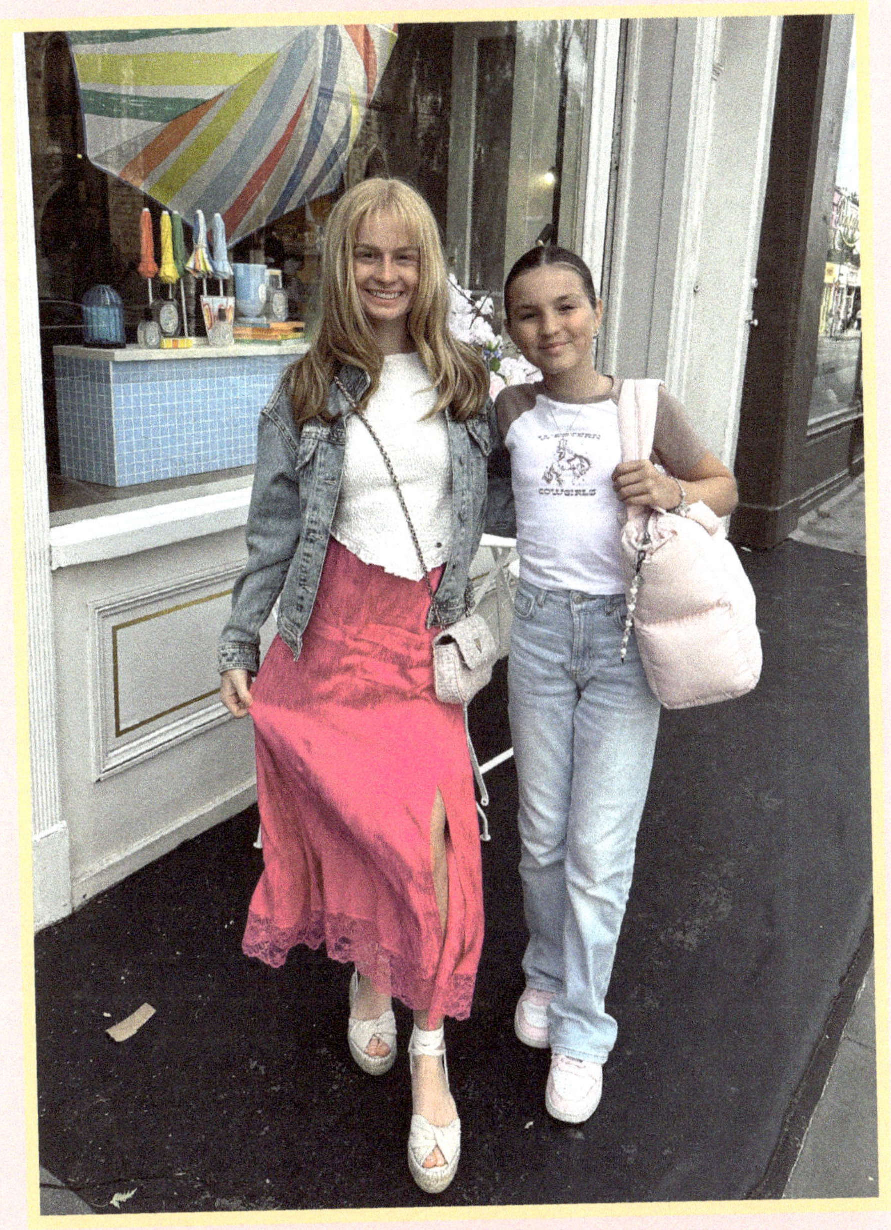

finding your passion

xoxo

8

M In primary school, I really wanted to learn the violin, so I begged my parents to have lessons. I did really enjoy it at first, and I'm glad that I had that experience, but pretty soon into it I realised that it just wasn't for me. And that's OK! Starting a new hobby can be hard, especially when it's something that requires a lot of skill, but you can't know if you'll enjoy something unless you give it a try. There have been a lot of hobbies that I've started, like crocheting and bouldering, which are my favourite now that I've practiced loads, but when I first tried, I definitely struggled and felt frustrated that I couldn't immediately make something off Pinterest or climb super-high grades. Trying something new requires patience and dedication, but you should still feel excited to progress, and when you do, because you went through starting from the beginning, it'll feel even more satisfying.

S I love all different types of hobbies, but my faves are definitely to do with art. I love art journaling, and I first found out about it through Pinterest. I really enjoy looking on Pinterest, and I think it's an amazing way to find ideas for all sorts of things! I have found so many nail art ideas, coconut girl bracelet inspo, things to draw in your sketchbook, art journal or clay art ideas, and much more. Art is even a fun way to make a gift for someone! I once found out we were going to see my aunt and nanny, and I didn't have a gift for them, so I made them a bracelet each, and they loved it. You could even sell things. Once, for my cheerleading fundraising, I sewed some cute little lavender bags. You don't just have to use the internet to find ideas; you can use books and magazines too. I have lots of different craft books that I like, and I love going to the library to find new ones. Sometimes I will even treat myself to a craft magazine when we go on holiday because it's so fun to try new ideas and different hobbies. If you want to find something you enjoy, or you want to try something new, ask a friend or family member if you can try their hobby with them. I don't really paint much, but Mia does a lot, and sometimes I join in with her, and it's actually super fun.

For a fun autumn-themed art challenge, we painted these pumpkins.

QUIZ

What Hobby Suits You

What would be your fave day trip?
- ✿ Try rock climbing
- ❖ Explore an art museum
- ♥ Look around a historical city
- ★ Go to a music concert

What would you most want to do on a rainy day stuck at home?
- ✿ Follow an at home workout
- ❖ Make a Pinterest-inspired collage
- ♥ Cuddle up with a book
- ★ Listen to your fave songs

When at a restaurant, do you pick food because it's:
- ✿ The healthiest and most filling
- ❖ The most interesting and creative dish
- ♥ The most aesthetic
- ★ World-famous

If you could go anywhere in the world, where would it be?
- ✿ Los Angeles
- ❖ Paris
- ♥ Rome
- ★ London

What would be your ideal vacation?
- ✿ Something active, like biking around a city or hiking in the mountains
- ❖ Visiting villages and getting demonstrations of the local craft
- ♥ Exploring the world's most famous monuments
- ★ Going to music events or shows every evening

RESULTS

Mostly ✿ You're super into sports and like getting active. Obviously, sports are important for everyone, but you should definitely try some more fun ones! There are so many different sports, but in the next chapter, we talk about all the ones we've tried.

Mostly ❖ You really appreciate art and getting creative for yourself. You could try painting and drawing, or more crafty things like crochet and jewellery making.

Mostly ♥ You're probably quite thoughtful and observant. Photography, reading, or writing could be the perfect hobbies for you.

Mostly ★ You're very musical. You could take singing lessons, learn an instrument, make electronic music, or dance. If you like putting on a performance, acting or theatre might be fun to try.

The best way to start a hobby is to, well, just start! It's easy to say, "Oh, I'd love to do this" or "I'd love to do that", but whether you're any good or even decide to keep at it, the main thing is to go out there and try. Obviously, some hobbies may require supplies, so see if any of your friends are into it and would let you borrow theirs, or go to a class trial to try it out. Another great thing is to use the internet! Discover new activities you never knew existed, find out what centres are in your area, or watch tutorial videos.

Ideas of hobbies:

- *Nail art* I absolutely suck at painting my nails, especially my right hand, so I definitely couldn't do anything fancy. However, I see so many girls online who are self-taught nail artists. You just have to be patient and start small.

- *Bracelet making* Sienna loves making bead bracelets, and she says it's really relaxing. You could also try making ones from string by braiding and tying knots.

- *Art journalling* This is so relaxing and a more creative take on your standard journalling. I love how all your art and what you've been up to is stored in one place, and it sounds so fun that you can look back on it.

- *Crochet and knitting* I really loved knitting when I was younger because my nanny taught me, but now I do a lot of crochet and love how versatile it is. I find it super relaxing but also incredibly exciting every time I finish a new project. There's so much you can make with crochet; the options are literally endless!

♥ *Macrame* I tried this while I was in Mexico, which is actually the birthplace of macrame. You start with a big stick (I loved getting driftwood from the beach for a natural look) and long pieces of thick yarn. You can then make so many different types of hanging art with knots.

♥ *Learn an instrument* Neither me nor Sienna have ever stuck at it, but I feel like it would be so rewarding and an amazing feeling to be able to make music yourself.

♥ *Learn a language* Ever since we lived in the Canary Islands, I have been working on my Spanish, and I hope to be fully fluent one day. It's especially fun once you start to pick some up and build enough confidence to know how to say things.

♥ *Acrylic, oil, or watercolour painting* The options with this are literally endless, and you can paint whatever suits your personal style and makes you feel inspired. I usually like to paint acrylic on canvas, but I love the idea of painting on other surfaces.

- ♥ *Wall murals* This is taking the last one to the next level. I've never tried spray paints, but it looks super fun. I see a lot of people on Instagram painting large murals with acrylic, too. Just make sure you're painting somewhere you're actually allowed to, haha!

- ♥ *Singing* Me and Sienna both have had singing lessons, but I think we realised we'd rather just do karaoke to our fave songs for fun and not worry about how we sound, haha!

- ♥ *Baking and cooking* I love trying new recipes and find food prep really relaxing. Plus, you get something to eat at the end of it!

- ♥ *Dance* One of my fave simple workouts is to blast my fave upbeat songs and dance as hard as I can. I'd love to take lessons or join a class and learn to dance properly one day.

- ♥ *Sketching and drawing* I love that it's so convenient to be able to do this any time. All you need is pencils and paper!

- ♥ *Journaling or writing* This is such a good way to reflect on what you've done or how you've been feeling. It's also really fun to use your imagination and try some creative writing!

- ♥ *Clay art* There's lots to make with this, and it's super relaxing!

finding your passion

S I've made rings and jewellery trays, then painted them once they dried to make them even cuter.

M

- *Sports* There are so many different sports you could try, all depending on what appeals to you and your fitness level. The next chapter is actually dedicated to sports, we love them so much.

- *Reading* This is a great way to learn new things, open your mind up to new ideas, and spark your imagination. I really like it for relaxing before bed.

M I drew this for you guys to colour in to help get your creative juices flowing.

finding your passion 129

in your sporty era

xoxo

9

S On Christmas, I asked my mum if I could do cheerleading classes. It sounded like a super-fun sport, and I knew lots of my friends did it. She agreed! I started in January, and I was a bit nervous at first, but all the girls on my team were super nice and made me feel welcome. Although I was a complete beginner at cheerleading, I had experience in gymnastics, so I ended up being the best on our team at tumbling (doing flips and other acrobatic moves). Two months after I joined, it was already competition time! The first comp that I entered with my team was surprisingly not the scariest, because I didn't put much pressure on myself to win. I just wanted to try my best and see how it would go. We ended up coming last out of six teams, lol!

S Six months later, it was the day of the summer final cheerleading competition. I was REALLY nervous for this competition, as me and my team had been working extra hard to do better than last time. When I walked into the venue where the competition was being held, I saw hundreds of cheerleaders from all different teams. I went to my team's area and said hi to my teammates. We did our hair in slick-back high ponytails with our cheer bows as we talked about our goals for the competition. We had one main goal: We wanted to be in the top three! Then we went to warm-up. All was going well until we did the "pyramid" (where the cheerleader is lifted high into the air by the other cheerleaders and they all have to link arms). I was in the air linking arms with the other flyers (a flyer is the cheerleader in the air), and one wobbled and fell, but her bases (bases hold the flyer) caught her, and because we were linking arms, she accidentally pulled me down too! I was suddenly falling and landed with a crash on my back. It really hurt! The coach immediately came rushing over to me asking if I needed ice. I said no, and she replied, "OK, get back up there"! It was so scary, but I had to pull myself together because we were about to go out to the stage! I did it one more time before a coach announced that it was time to come out on stage. We were the second team to perform, so we really didn't have long to prepare. When it was our turn, I looked out at the audience and saw my parents smiling and waving at me. We said our cheer chant, which is:

> *"Black and white, we're here to fight.*
> *Our jumps are tight, our stunts take flight.*
> *We are the wolves, we're here to win.*
> *We are the best, we ain't messin"!*

After we said our chant, we got into the opening position and began our routine. It went really well, I didn't fall or mess up, and I even waved to the crowd when I was up in the air. My team and I just waited and watched the other performances. They were all really good, and we began to wonder if we could even come in fifth. Finally, everyone had finished their routine, and each team sat on the stage in a circle. We crossed our fingers and linked arms as the hall went silent.

"In third place is . . . **the Wolves!**"

S   We had placed! We all squealed with excitement and hugged each other as the medals were placed around our necks. I was so happy but also a bit sad, as this was to be my last time cheerleading with the team, as I had decided to focus solely on gymnastics. I think cheerleading is a very difficult but super-fun sport, and I am still so proud of myself and my team that we won bronze!

Me with my medal and bouquet after placing!

M Ever since I was a little kid, I've always gotten so excited whenever I saw a climbing wall, so when I was thirteen, I started going to a teen bouldering group every week. It was so fun and great exercise at the same time! Eventually, I fell out of the habit of going to climbing centres, and because I didn't have a specific sport I was trying to get better at, it made exercise seem so much more of a chore, because I knew I was only doing it to keep fit. So in 2023, I decided that I'd had enough of barely exercising and feeling like I found it too hard to do and joined a bouldering gym. It was definitely scary at first because I felt like a complete beginner, as it had been so long, and I knew I needed to build up a lot of strength to be able to reach my goals in climbing. After going a couple times, I started to feel way more confident and realised how much I love it. Finding a sport that I enjoy mentally and feels good for my body not only has helped encourage me to keep fit and healthy but has given me a sense of satisfaction and more purpose for working out. Now, when I go to the gym, I know the more I push myself, the stronger I'll become, so I can climb harder grades. It's also motivated me to challenge myself with new sports.

S When I was five, I first found out about gymnastics, and it sounded like a fun way for me to let out my endless energy, so I joined a class for about three months. After that, I tried some other sports like parkour and skateboarding, and even though I did enjoy them, I still wanted to find a sport that felt perfect for me. When we moved to London, I decided to give gymnastics another try, as I knew there were some really good clubs in England, and it sounded really fun! I started the week before my eleventh birthday, so I have been doing it for over two years now, and I love it! I really enjoy gymnastics because it has the perfect combo of strength, flexibility, and grace. Although I love pretty much every sport, gymnastics is the best for me.

> *"Was it difficult starting gymnastics when you were considered older?"* **BY TAYLOR**

S Most gymnasts start gymnastics around four or five years old, but I started a week before my eleventh birthday, so I am definitely a late beginner. I have now been doing gymnastics for two years, but I can do the same things as my friends who have been doing it for eight years, because I progressed quickly. I have definitely put in lots of work and effort, but I think the most important thing is to enjoy yourself. Because I enjoy gymnastics, I don't mind having to put in all the hours. Although I do sometimes wish I started earlier, I'm super happy I'm at the level I'm at. xoxo

M Keeping active is so important for overall health, and the more you do it, the easier it becomes. If you want to start being more active but find it overwhelming, don't worry: a lot of people feel that way. I'd recommend starting with something which sounds fun to you, like going swimming, biking to a cool location with a friend, or going to a trampoline park! The more exercise you do, the easier it becomes, so the most important thing is that you take action and start today. Choose to walk somewhere you'd usually drive to, or if your parents/friends do a sport, ask to go along with them one time.

S A great way to do exercise more often is to go to a weekly class or meet up with a sports group. It's very important to enjoy exercising. If you hate it, you're not likely to do it every day!

But if you really like a sport and you have a weekly class, it will be something you'll look forward to. Also, when you join a club, it's an amazing way to make friends, as you already have something in common: your sport!

Here are some sports we've tried:

- *Skateboarding* I never thought I'd be able to skateboard, or even want to. It sounded so scary and difficult to balance on some wheels, haha! But in 2021, Sienna got super into it and was obsessed with Sky Brown (who's an Olympic skateboarder), and I saw her trying to skate all the time. I decided to try it for myself as a joke, and absolutely fell on my butt. After that, I realised how fun it could be, so I decided to try to teach myself. It took a LONG time just to be able to ride on flat ground, but I didn't give up, and I eventually learnt to do a drop-in.

- *Surfing* I had one lesson on surfing with Sienna . . . and pretty quickly decided that it wasn't something I was interested in. I'm just not the biggest fan of getting loads of salt water in my eyes and nose. That's not to say I won't try it again, and I probably will! I think when I tried, I didn't have as much lower body strength, so it was harder to keep on the board, so I think it would be a good challenge for me.

Us at the skatepark in Costa Rica

in your sporty era **137**

Playing tennis with our mum in London.

- ♥ *Hiking* This is probably one of my favourite sports, and I always try to go on a long walk every day. I love going on proper hikes on nature trails when I can. The feeling of being on foot in nature is so fun, like a proper adventure. I think it's a really good sport if you're just getting started or if you want something more relaxing.

- ♥ *Tennis* We've only played tennis a couple of times, as our parents like to go, but I definitely want to practise more! I think it's great cardio and love the competitive aspect.

- ♥ *Climbing* Actually, bouldering is definitely my favourite sport. I love how versatile it is, as I mostly do indoor bouldering, but there are a lot of different types of climbing you can do with ropes and even outdoors! I love how each climb is like a different puzzle for the mind and body, and it's really good for both! I definitely recommend that everyone try it, lol!

- ♥ *Skiing* Because I'd already learnt to skateboard, I felt confident that I'd be able to pick up the basics pretty quickly. That's not to say it wasn't absolutely terrifying! The feeling of racing down a snowy mountain is definitely unique, and maybe not for everyone, but me and Sienna LOVE it.

When we went skiing in Switzerland.

💗 *Running* I have been doing more running recently, and I love how it makes me feel empowered and clears my mind. It's like meditation for me! I've run some 5Ks, and I definitely want to keep setting myself running goals to work on. It's also probably the easiest sport to start, since all you need is trainers, and you can control the difficulty for your level by how fast and far you go.

💗 *Obstacle courses* In 2024, because I'd been doing a lot of running training, I decided to see if I could take it to the next level. I booked myself into a Tough Mudder race without any research into what obstacles it actually has, and I'm so glad I did! It was an amazing experience, and we actually vlogged the whole experience on our YouTube channel, Fizzier, so if you want to see what it was like, go check that out! I'm definitely going to be doing more in the future.

After I finished my Tough Mudder!

S **I've also tried a few more sports that Mia hasn't:**

- ♥ *Parkour* I went to a kid's group for a while when I was little and really enjoyed it. I've always been the kid who climbed doorframes and stair rails, so at parkour, I got to climb and jump loads, which I loved.

- ♥ *Cheerleading* I loved it, but unfortunately, in England, where I had lessons, they don't use pom-poms like they do in the American movies.

- ♥ *Gymnastics* AKA my favourite sport ever!

Mia's At-Home 10-Minute Workout

I love doing this on a day when I don't have much time or I'm feeling lethargic. Just set a timer on your phone and give yourself some space. There are adaptations to make it easier for beginners or to make it harder if you want more of a challenge.

45 seconds: squats

To add more cardio, try jump squats.
You can also hold a weight to make it harder.

15 SECONDS REST

45 seconds: push-ups

If you can't do full ones, try from on your knees.

15 SECONDS REST

45 seconds: donkey kicks

Keep alternating between each leg.

15 SECONDS REST

45 seconds: glute bridge

15 SECONDS REST

45 seconds: plank hold

15 SECONDS REST

Repeat and feel proud of yourself!

learning & growing

xoxo

10

I have tried a lot of different types of schooling methods, and my favourite was definitely being homeschooled. Up until Year 5, I went to my local primary school, but then we moved to a new area that didn't have any space available for me at the schools. So me and my parents decided to try homeschooling. I loved it because I got to really focus on my passions, like researching everything about the ancient Greeks and Romans, knitting, and creative writing. I actually started a blog, so after I learnt about something, I'd write an article about it, which was a really good way for me to showcase what I was working on and currently doing in my life. I'm pretty sure only my aunt read it, but I had so much fun writing, and it's because of the blog that I actually started YouTube! I'm so glad that I have it all to look back on; it's so cute and nostalgic for me to read now. Here's one of my old blog posts from 2015:

My Second Ever Race!!!

Posted on June 22, 2015 by Mia

Hi guys! Last Wednesday I ran my second ever race which was 1k race for year 5 and 6 girls.

Me before my race

We got the bus to get there and when we arrived I had to wait for the other years to race – including the pre-school children's race which my three year old sister ran!

When it was finally time for my race I started doing some warm ups which were some short laps around the field and some bum kicks.

Then it was time for the final thing. I lined up on the start line and got ready to go. The horn went and I started running. On the last stretch I sprinted as fast as I could.

Me at the start line

After my race I went to the local Tescos which only 5 minutes away. I got about 50 peaches(they weren't all for me though!) for 46p.

I really enjoyed it and it was great fun!

I did enjoy public school, too, and I think it's important to try your best in anything you do in life. At the same time, I think the mainstream school system is definitely not designed with every child in mind, and just because someone doesn't necessarily have the best grades, it doesn't mean that they're "dumb" or not going to succeed in life. Besides, everyone grows up at different rates, and just because someone is super quick at learning something doesn't mean it's better. After all, Einstein didn't speak until he was five, according to some biographers. Everyone has different talents, and I find the idea of someone who had the potential to be talented in a way that's not classed as "academic" feeling like they're not able to express themselves properly really upsetting. I know there can be a lot of pressure to get certain grades, but ultimately, school is meant to be about learning. And learning can and should be fun! If you do have an exam coming up and want to try your best on it, here are some tips from Sienna:

S

♥ Sometimes I find that **a reward is what keeps me going**. It can be something simple like a bar of chocolate, watching an episode of your fave show, or jumping on your trampoline. Set a timer or a certain amount of work you have to do before you can have the reward. I saw a really cool idea of getting a candle and putting it in a cupcake. Study until the candle runs out, and at the end, you get the reward of eating the cupcake! You could also fill a glass with ice and study until all the ice has melted. This way, you get lots of work done, but it feels fun and very satisfying at the end!

- Another tip I have is to **do the subject you least like first**, and then it's done and out of the way, so you are not left with a giant pile of your least favourite subject.

- I also really **like studying outside**, so if you are allowed, go to your garden, local park, or the beach, and study there. It's actually really relaxing, and it makes it easier to study. If you can't go out in nature, then you could go to your local library or cafe.

- **Studying with someone else** is a great way to make learning actually enjoyable. You could plan a meetup with some of your friends at your house and all study together. It's nice because you can help each other out, whether you are in the same year or not.

- **Try playing some study music or ambient sounds.** This can help with focus, and it's also really relaxing.

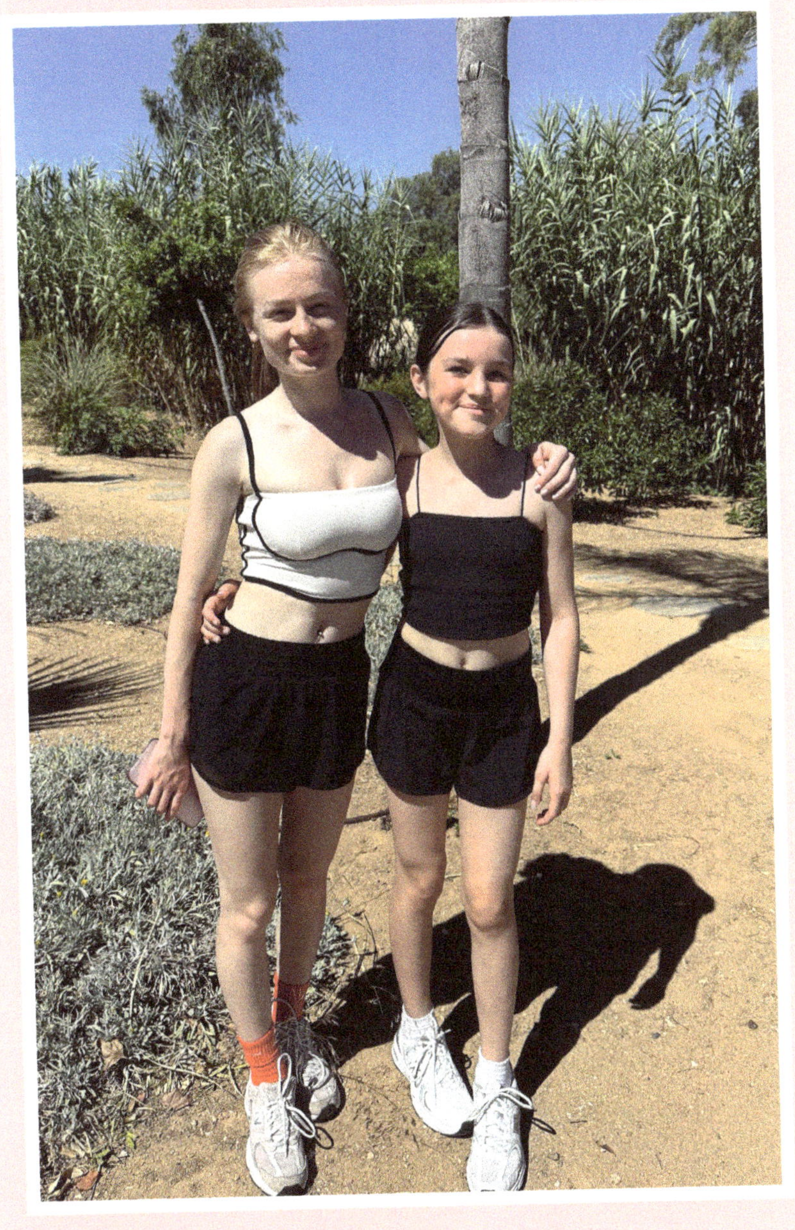

M My favourite way to learn is actually self-learning. For example, I love learning about the chakras and Ayurvedic medicine, so my dad gave me a book written by a lady who is an expert on the practises and mantras. I wrote lots of notes as I was reading, and then did more research from other books and online. I knew I wanted to compile all the information I'd learnt somehow because I felt so inspired, so I got to painting! I made a layered painting where each section is dedicated to a chakra, and every element in it has a meaning behind it, with the element that corresponds, the colour, and the mantra.

M I feel like making or writing something out of all the information you've learnt is the best way to really understand and remember it. I've made PowerPoints before or posters and given a presentation of them to my parents, and I also recapped what I learnt in my blog posts and YouTube videos!

learning & growing

Challenge

I want you to thoroughly research and learn about something you find interesting.

There's probably a lot you might have been wanting to research for a while! For example, you could learn about the back story of your favourite music artist and find out why they became a musician. What inspires them? Why do they like to make that genre of music? What is their process for making a song?

Then, I want you to make a project **showcasing all that you learnt**. Everyone has different abilities and interests, so there are many different ways you could do this. You could make some **scrapbook** pages showcasing what you learnt, do some **creative writing** inspired on their life, **make a song** about them, or do some **fan art** with significant meaning to them. If you prefer more analytical things, you could **write an educational article** or **speech**.

The main thing is that you feel inspired and excited about learning and creating!

S   A good project you could do is to start learning a language you don't know a single word of but you might have always wanted to learn. There are lots of different ways to learn, like with Duolingo or Memrise, which are great language learning apps; workbooks (they can really help with grammar and spelling); and YouTube videos.

All the ways we know how to say hello in different languages:

Hola - Spanish
Olá - Portuguese
Ciao - Italian
Nĭ hăo - Chinese
Kon'nichiwa - Japanese
Aloha - Hawaiian
Hallo - German
Buna – Romanian

Write your own here:
_____ - _____
_____ - _____
_____ - _____

learning & growing

> *I'm going into year 10 this year, and I still don't know what I want to do for a job. Is that OK?*
> BY JASMIN

M That's definitely okay! While it is important and makes life more exciting to have goals, you definitely don't need to have super long-term goals or feel like you're stuck and not allowed to change interests. Part of life is discovering what you like, especially while you're growing up, so I'd recommend just focusing on what excites and motivates you, but don't be shy about trying something different. It's totally normal to not be sure yet, so don't stress. xoxo

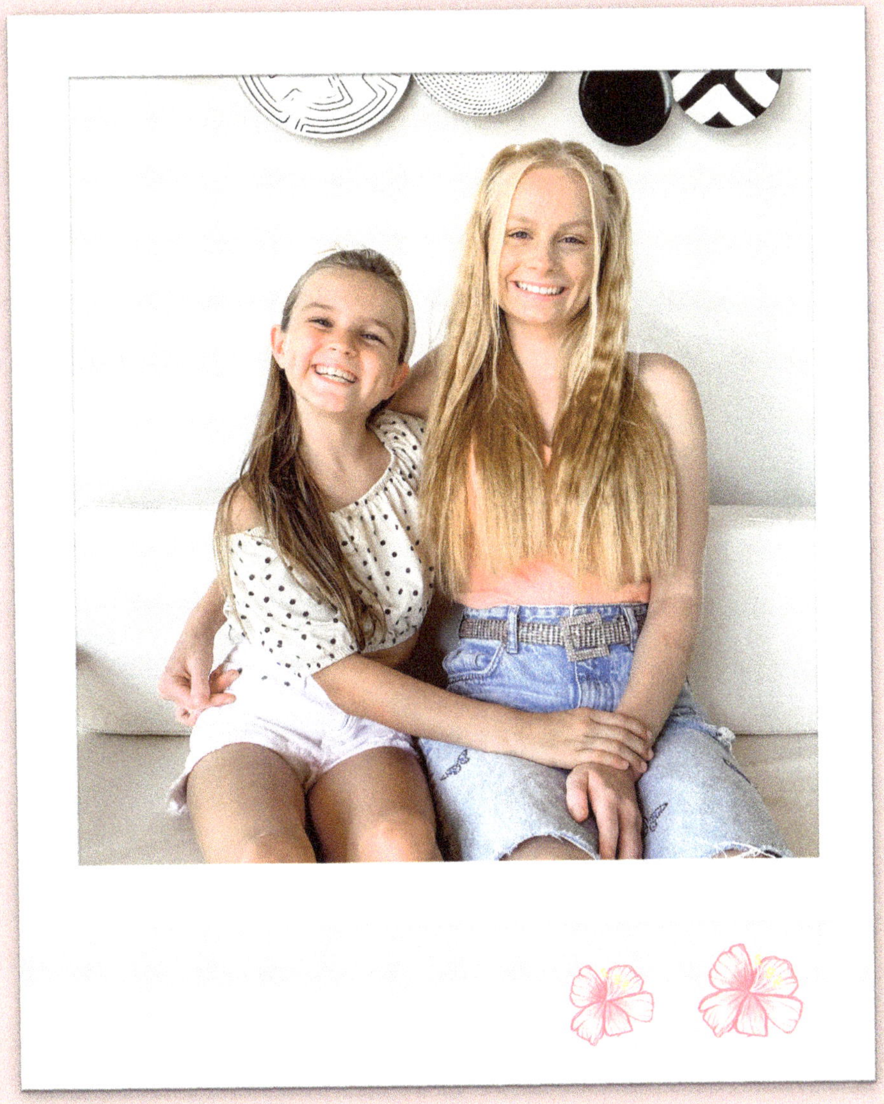

travel to grow

While on holiday in Dubai, UAE, we did a photoshoot out in the desert. It was so beautiful.

11

I love travelling, and it's more than just seeing the world's most iconic tourist spots (even though that is super cool). I love it because it forces you to get out of your comfort zone and try new things and new foods and live life differently from your normal routine. There are so many different ways to travel nowadays, and I feel so grateful that I get to live in this world that's all interconnected, because I can't imagine what it must've been like for past generations when you couldn't even get avocados in the UK!

S

Here are some of my favourite photos from our travels:

This is us coming home from an amazing two-week trip in Spain.

In 2024 we went on a safari in Botswana, Africa. It was so epic, and we saw so many animals, even two lions super up close!

While we were in Botswana, we went canoeing along a river, but it was very scary because we could hear hippos in the bushes right next to us!

This is the iconic Durdle Door in Dorset, England.
We went for a really fun hike and then had a picnic
on the beach, and the sea was freezing!

We went for an autumn trip to New York! It was so cool; we saw all of the iconic sights, including the Statue of Liberty and the Empire State Building.

In 2019 we went to Bali, Indonesia. We had so much fun sipping coconuts and sunbathing!

This was at our parents' wedding in the Grand Canyon! It was one of the best moments ever. We even flew in a helicopter.

This is a Mayan pyramid that we visited in Mexico. It was so big!

We had so much fun hanging out at the pool in Portugal. We also went camping in the garden. It was so surreal sleeping under the stars.

We went to Disneyland in California. We look so cute standing outside the Disney castle in our Mickey Mouse ears.

We went to the top of Tower Bridge in London, England.

M Flying is so fun, but it can get quite tiring and tedious. **Here are some things I love to do to help keep it an enjoyable experience:**

- **Don't overthink!** As with anything in life that can be a bit scary, if you know that you'd love to do it but start thinking of all the ways it could (highly unlikely) go wrong, it will hold you back so much. Make sure to keep yourself distracted, and don't focus on anything which is to do with the risks (aka, negative films).

- Prepare some things to keep yourself entertained, like **downloaded movies**, **books**, and **activity sheets**.

- If you're flying at night, **bring things that make you feel cosy**. I really like lavender or ylang ylang essential oil.

- Flying can get a bit sweaty, and it feels really nice to be able to keep fresh. **Don't forget your toothbrush!** You could get some **natural wet wipes** and **water spray** to help you keep clean.

- My skin can get really dry from flying, so I always like to bring some **facial oil** or **natural moisturiser**.

- I absolutely hate it when my ears pop, and sometimes it can be quite painful! Bring some **gum** or **mints** to use during take-off and landing.

- It's really important to stay hydrated during a flight. If you struggle, try adding some fruit to your water to make it taste nicer, or set a timer for every twenty minutes to remind yourself to drink more.

- You need to keep your blood flowing, and sitting down for long periods takes a big toll on the body. Try to do walks up and down the aisle, take the stairs when you can in the airports, and see if you can fit in a workout on the day you travel. Even if you only do ten minutes, it's better than not doing anything!

S   I love to go on staycations to my grandparents' or auntie's house because it feels like I'm going on holiday, even though I'm only a few hours' drive from home! I also love going on vacations in different countries because it's super fun to explore new places, try new food, and learn new languages.

M   You definitely don't have to go abroad to travel, and you don't even need to go too far either. I feel like often when I live in a place, I'll end up seeing less than if I was only there for a week's holiday. The key is to actually take the time and put in effort to go and see new things. You could look online for activities to do near you or ask family and friends; you never know what might have been in front of you this whole time! If you want to explore new cultures, you also don't have to travel far. You could look online for recipes or see if you have any restaurants or shops with that cuisine near you.

S   I love road trips! But even though they are super fun, being stuck in a car for five hours can sometimes get a bit boring, so I've made the perfect list of things to do out on the open road:

- *Listen to music, audiobooks, or a podcast* You can get the whole car dancing with you, or it's really nice to use headphones. Also, you could listen to a relaxing story or song to help you fall asleep.

- *Try new snacks or make food combos* I **LOVE** snacks! And you might not believe me, but chocolate and spicy crisps actually taste really good together (or maybe I was just really hungry, lol).

M Eww! Why on earth did you even eat that, Sienna?

S

- 💗 *Use a face mask / do your skincare* Cars can really dry your skin out, so this is really good for it, but also super fun.

- 💗 *Take funny selfies* This is a hilarious activity. Don't forget to do some on 0.5!

- *Draw* Although the car can make things a bit bumpy, I really like drawing on a road trip because you can make scenic pictures.

- *Make an out-the-window scavenger hunt* Pre car journey, get a piece of paper and write out all the different things you think you might see from the car. You could even make one for the other passengers and have a competition to see who will find all the things on the list first!

- *Watch a downloaded video or movie* To make a cozy setup, you could bring a blanket and pillow, some popcorn, and your fave plushie!

- *Read a magazine or book (this one!)* I love reading, but you do have to be careful not to feel carsick!

- *Play truth or dare with the other passengers* You could even do the dares when you have a pit stop.

- *Buy something nice to open in the car* This is really fun because you have something new to look forward to. It could be a colouring book, craft kit, or beauty product.

- *Make a travel journal* This is a super-fun way to remember your trip. Get a notebook and write about what you do on your trip. Stick in different things, like a map of where you're going, postcards, tickets, and photos.

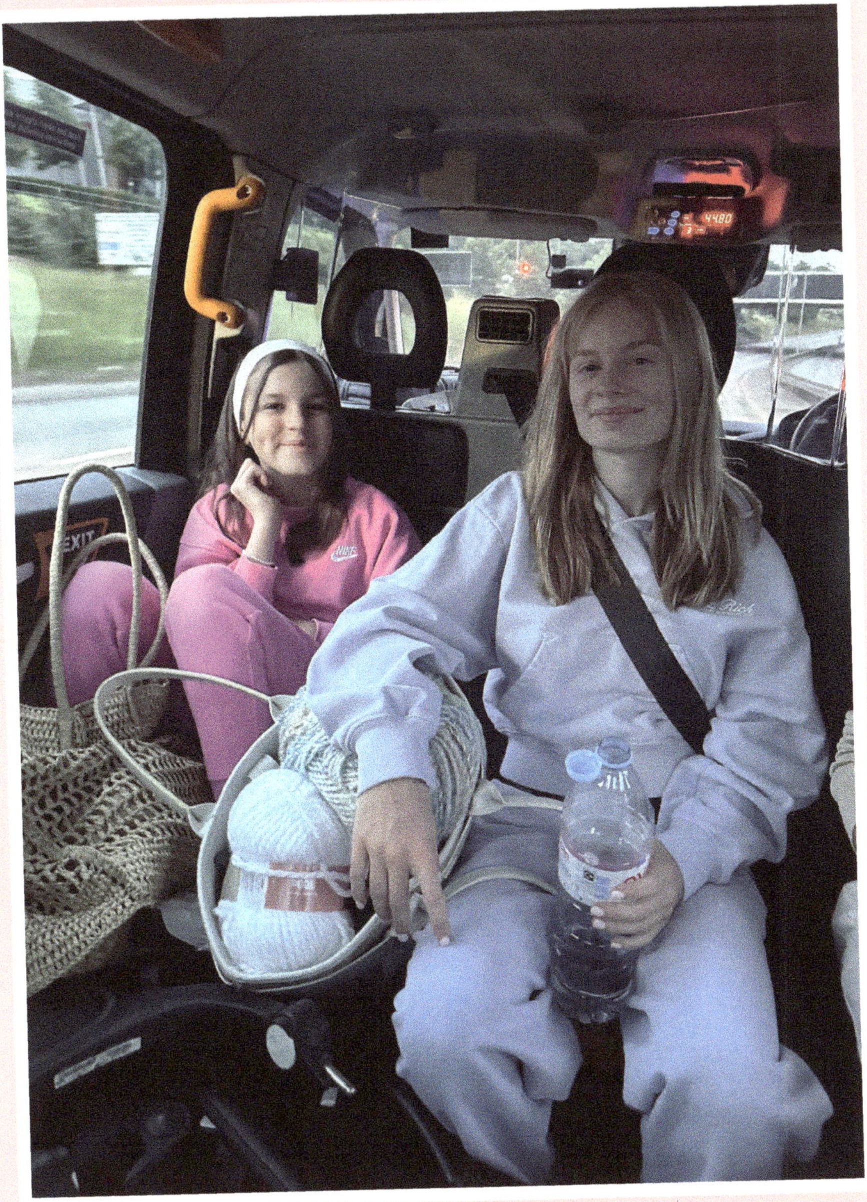
EXIT

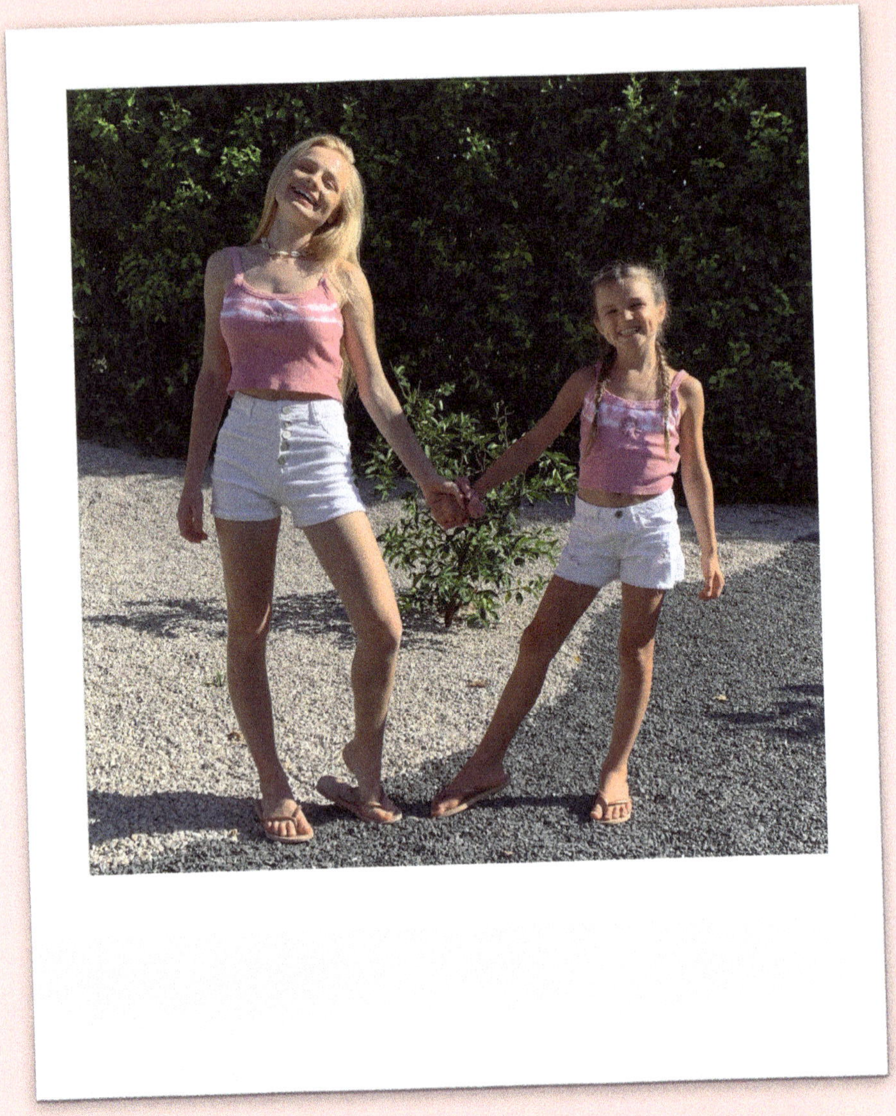

the end...

And you've made it to the end of our book! Thanks so much for always supporting us and taking the time to read this. We love hearing your stories and feedback, so please leave us a message on our social media or a review on Amazon and let us know if you've enjoyed this book. I'm so excited to see everyone who's reading it!

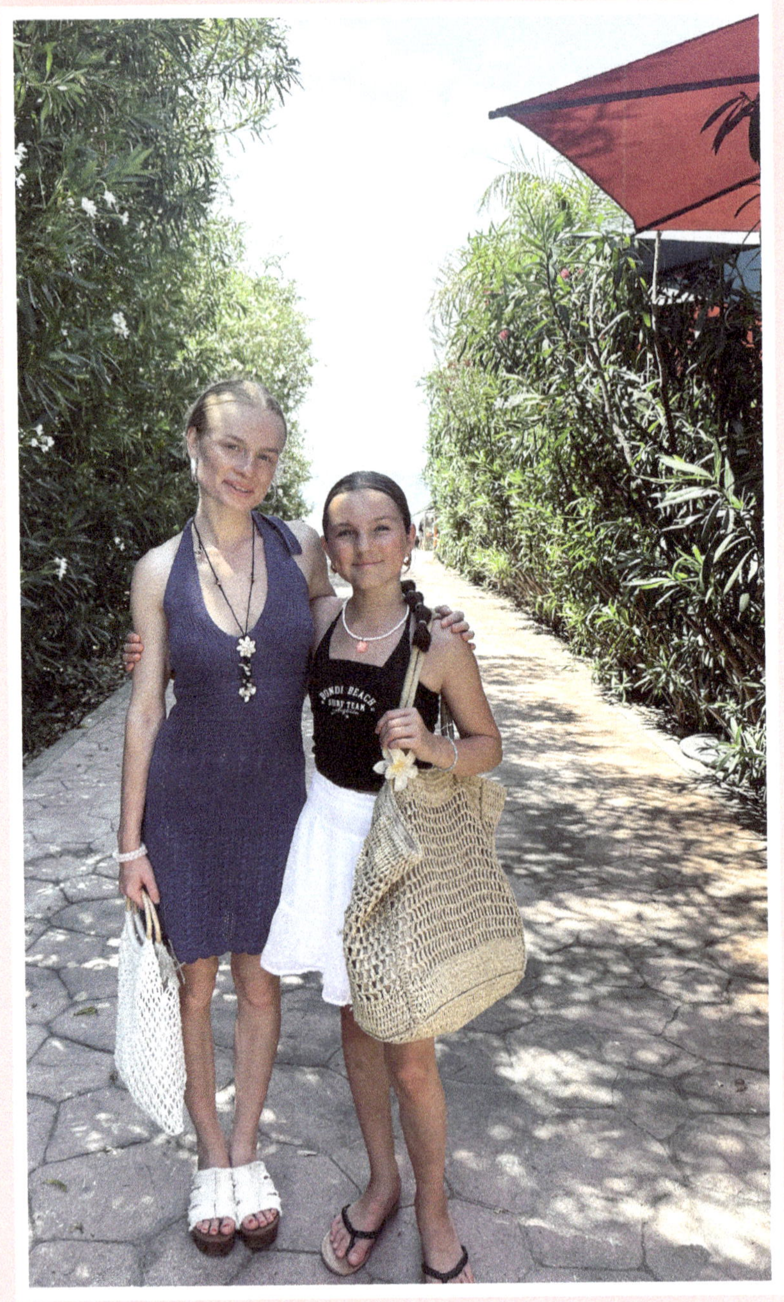
BONDI BEACH
SURF TEAM

S Thank you so much for reading all of our book. To be honest, I actually can't believe Mia and I managed to write this entire thing! I'm so happy that you guys are now finally able to read it.

Also, big thanks to our lovely photographer, Lauren Marsh. The photoshoot was so fun!

Thanks to our amazing editor, Grammargal, and our book designer, Anna Perotti.

Until next time,

Byeeeeeee x

Mia & Sienna

xoxo